Out
S

Did something experiment

Fred.

Fred J. Fischer

The
White Trash
River Boys

Casting About for the
Meaning of Life

Library of Congress Cataloging-in-Publication Data
Fischer, Fred, J.
  The White Trash River Boys / Fred J. Fischer
        p.   cm.
     ISBN 1453719423
     1. Camping—Humor
     2. Fishing—Missouri
     3. Nature—Religious aspects
     I. Title

Fred J. Fischer
Columbia, Mo. 65203
fredjfischer@yahoo.com

Cover photos of the Osage River by Russell Kuttenkuler.

Contents

Acknowledgments

Thank you for the fun and friendship, my five White Trash Boys; my brother Paul, the three Kuttenkuler brothers, Bob, Russ and Mike and my friend and neighbor Gene Hrdina. My greatest thanks, of course, must go to my wife, Janet. Without your love, friendship and support none of this would have happened.

vi

CHAPTER ONE

The First Year

I believe there is a special mystery that can be experienced sitting around a fire. By mystery, I mean the Native American interpretation of the word. Mystery meaning something related to the spiritual. Most people are probably more familiar with using the word "medicine"—as we remember from the movies and television shows of our youth (as in "medicine man"). Regardless of how citified a person may be, I believe anyone who stares into the restless flames and skittering heat of the embers and logs of a campfire knows that feeling of mystery. As a culture we continue to pay homage to this mystery by including fireplaces in our homes. In the modern, schizophrenic mind, we have gone so far as to bottle up the flames behind a glass panel, install logs that never burn, pipe in fossil fuel and called it a gas fireplace. I can think of no better example of how modern humans embrace and reject their true nature simultaneously.

That observation may seem a little too deep for a man who considers himself just a working class guy. Growing up on a farm may make my roots a little less citified than the typical person but almost all of us are only a grandparent or great-grandparent away from the soil. As a modern American I do what most all of us do; get up every morning, go to work, come home, eat supper, watch TV, go to bed and get up the next morning and do it all over. Since I grew up in a rural area there was time in my youth for squirrel hunting, swimming in ponds, picking blackberries, wandering over plowed fields hunting for arrowheads and lying on gravel bars in the sunshine. Adulthood, for me at least, seemed to slowly squeeze out these things. I began to suffer from an affliction that I believe is common in modern culture, lack of exposure to the mystery of the great outdoors.

My wife, Janet, and I have been self-employed for many years and have enjoyed annually hosting a bratwurst-beer-German potato salad, Octoberfest party. Business associates, friends and family are invited to help us remember our German heritage. The beginning of the White Trash River Boys dates from one of those Octoberfest parties a few years back. As is typical for October, the weather was mild and sunny but as night came on the temperature began to fall so a bonfire was started in our yard. The party dwindled down to the last dozen or so who stayed to enjoy the clear night and help try to kill the keg. Staring into the fire, I began to feel that mystery. All around were smiling, rosy-illuminated faces, above, the black sky punctuated by silver points, below, the soft yielding grass and behind us the increasingly sharp chill of a dark, clear autumn evening. I had been reading an abridged version of the *Journals of Lewis and Clark* and began to share some of their exploits with the others around the fire. Present with us that night was my old hometown friend Russ. While in college we had enjoyed a couple of Ozark river floating trips together but now this busy stage of adulthood seemed to leave little time for such activities. The Lewis and Clark tales reminded Russ of a recent article in the *St. Louis Post-Dispatch* of two guys who had floated in a canoe down the Missouri River from its beginning at the confluence of the Jefferson, Gallatin and Madison Rivers to where it joins the Mississippi at St. Louis. That grand adventure caused a small idea to surface that had been floating around in the back of my mind for some time. The State of Missouri is well known for its namesake river that flows across the middle of the state. And most Americans who remember their grade school geography realize that the Mississippi River forms the eastern border. The third largest river is the Osage, named after the powerful nation that once controlled almost its entire drainage basin in Missouri and Kansas. Midwesterners are more likely to be familiar with the river in its dammed versions, The Lake of the Ozarks and Truman Lake. I knew the Osage below Bagnell Dam flowed through, what in my opinion, is the most beautiful part of the State. Once I had asked my father-in-law if he had fished that part of the river. "Yes," he had said, "the fishing was good." He added, "It is an easy float from Bagnell Dam to the Missouri River."

So a small idea bobbed in my head as I listened to the quiet conversations around that Octoberfest bonfire. Not wanting to discuss my idea in front of the other guests, I waited for the fire to burn down and then asked Russ to help me carry another load from the woodpile. Away from the fire, standing in the suddenly cold night air, we paused for a moment to enjoy the gorgeous stars.

"Russ," I blurted out without any preamble, "I've been thinking that you and I ought to get a boat and float the Osage River from Bagnell Dam to the Missouri River." Having never actually said the thought out loud before and after comparing it to Lewis and Clark and those other two guys in the canoe, I thought the suddenly lame idea seemed to sink heavily in the quiet air.

It was too dark to see Russ' face. He dropped the two logs he was holding and straightened up and took a moment to look at the stars again. Then he said, "With beautiful weather like this we should go as soon as possible. I know

I'm busy next weekend but could we go the first weekend in November?"

The next weekend I began to work on getting my equipment together. The main problem I had at this point was that I didn't have a boat, motor, tent, sleeping bag, camp cooking equipment, fishing pole or tackle box. There was an old aluminum rowboat and 1950's era outboard motor at my family's cabin at the Lake of the Ozarks. I drove down in my pickup to get them. While I was there I scrounged around in the basement and found an unclaimed and only slightly broken down fishing pole. I "liberated" small amounts of lures, hooks, weights, etc. from several tackle boxes stored there—hopefully just enough not to be noticed by my family members.

I used to have quite a good collection of camping equipment. I sold it in a garage sale when my wife announced after a couple years of marriage that she really did not like camping. At that time, I got rid of it without remorse since I was caught up in a life of working hard and believed that I'd never really find time to use that stuff again. I remembered that there was an old sleeping bag with a broken zipper in my mother's attic. My father had bought it in 1961 to accompany my brother on a Future Farmers of America trip out West. Russ told me he had a tent so I didn't have to chase down my old tent that I had lent to my brother-in-law. After digging on hands and knees through the dark recesses of our kitchen cabinets I came up with several banged up pots and pans that could serve as the cooking gear I'd need.

Since I was reasonably sure that old Royal outboard motor had not been run for 20 years, when I got it home I clamped it to a saw horse, submerged the prop in a trash can full of water, filled the gas tank and began pulling on the starting rope. After 10 pulls—probably a good idea to clean and check the spark plug. After another 10 pulls—probably a good idea to check to see if gas is getting to the carburetor. After another 10 pulls—better double check to make sure there aren't any hidden switches or valves that are in the "off" position. After about a hundred pulls my arm was flaccid at my side and my shoulder was twitching from shots of lightening coursing towards my neck. The entire top of the motor was disassembled and I had reached the end of my physical and mental abilities. As I slowly began to put the pieces back together on the quiet motor I was reminded of an old McCullough chainsaw we had when I was growing up. That thing was the hardest starting gas engine ever designed. My uncle who lived on the farm just next to us had one just like ours and he said it took two able bodied men to use it. The first man would wind the starter cord and pull, wind and pull, wind and pull for an hour until it finally started running. He would then go lie down in the truck and rest while the other man cut the firewood.

Now I was in a dilemma, we were floating next weekend and I had a boat but no motor. I was reasonably sure we did not want to paddle our way downstream because I thought I knew the Osage River well enough to believe there were long wide sections where there would be almost no current. I didn't have enough time to take the old Royal to a shop to be serviced and I sure as heck was not going to spend $1,000 to buy a new outboard motor. At that point I fell back on a personal rule of thumb. If you need something and you don't have a lot of money to spend, go to Wal-Mart. I wasn't sure what they could do for me but I knew they had a fishing equipment department. Once there, I discovered a 12 volt battery powered trolling motor that looked like what might be my answer. Motor plus a 12 volt battery came to just under $400. Now I can tell you I spent a very long time pacing up and down the aisle in the store trying to justify spending 400 bucks. I hadn't been much for fishing in the past so I didn't really expect that after this one time float of the Osage River I'd have much use for the motor. I could use the battery in my truck. The one I had there was four years old and was likely to conk out in the next couple of years anyway. I was up against the wall time wise and if I didn't use the trolling motor again, maybe I could sell it in the newspaper and recover some of my investment. So I swallowed hard, took out my credit card and made my purchase.

I spent the last hour before bed Thursday night pouring over a highway map. I was trying to get an idea of how many miles our trek would be. We would put in at a campground just below Bagnell Dam and take out at a Department of Conservation boat ramp, called the Mari-Osa Delta Access, just outside of Jefferson City. That was still about 15 miles from where the Osage ran into the Missouri River but since we'd only have a trolling motor I did not want to get anywhere near the Big Mo. It looked to me to be about a 50 mile float. I studied the owner's manual for the trolling motor. I did some crude calculations involving miles, estimated current speed, amp consumption, etc. and began to fear that one battery might not provide enough juice. I called my father-in-law to borrow his deep cycle marine battery. Then I asked him about a 50 mile float in two days. "No problem," he said. Then I mentioned that we'd only be using a trolling motor—silence on the other end, then, "You boys might be biting off more than you can chew."

Launch Friday dawned cloudy and in the low twenties. The forecast for the weekend included possible light showers. I still had shopping and packing to do so I took the entire day off. I told Russ I'd supply all the food. He should bring just his personal snacks and beverages. A quick run to the grocery store and I was back home. The first step in getting my clothes together was to replace the coat that I had planned to take with a heavier one. I double checked to make sure my rain gear and old tennis shoes were included. I would wear the old tennis shoes if the river turned out to be shallow in places. If so, we'd get out of the boat and push it across the gravel. Food, beer, water, etc. went into the cooler and most everything else into plastic trash bags. Not being familiar with this river, I was not taking any chances. The trash bag technique is a common procedure when canoeing on smaller Ozark streams. It keeps things dry from the general dampness in the bottom of the canoe, the bagged items are protected in case of rain and most things float awhile if the canoe turns over. Since it was now November, I did not enjoy thinking about the possibility of our rowboat turning over, but I thought it would be best to respect the old Boy Scout motto, "Be Prepared."

I was meeting Russ at 3 PM at the take-out boat ramp where he would leave his car so that at the end of our float we would have a vehicle to shuttle back to the put-in where I left my truck. After lunch, I loaded the aluminum boat in the back of my pickup. The bow was sticking out the rear about four feet. I tied a red flag on its front handle. Soon the inside of the boat was filled with what I hoped would be everything we'd need. By 1:30 I was heading down my driveway.

After a quick stop at my father-in-law's for the battery, I arrived at the boat ramp 15 minutes early. I wandered around the vacant parking lot.

It was a cold, cloudy November day. It didn't seem to be real popular fishing weather. As I wandered, I found a strap used for towing cars. It was a good quality nylon strap with a strong hook on each end. Quite a good find!

I was a little surprised when our meeting time came and went and no Russ. He's one of the most conscientious individuals I know. After about 45 minutes a beat-up old car pulled in the lot. Behind the wheel was an old man and in the passenger side was Russ. He stepped out and thanked the old guy who then circled the lot and drove off. After a brief hello, Russ said his car was broken down about 40 miles east. After discussing several options, I remembered the tow rope I had just found. We had to go back to get his equipment anyway, so why not use my truck to tow his car to a service station in one of the little towns along the way?

When we got to his car we did spend a few moments staring morosely under the hood of the Escort hoping we could fix the problem. I got a few tools out from behind my truck seat but since we didn't really know what we were doing, that effort did not last long. Soon we were on our way with Russ steering his car at the end of the tow strap. The strap was about 16' long and by time you hooked it on both bumpers that placed the front of Russ's car about 8' from the bow of my boat. I promised to keep my speed less than 30 miles per hour and with a gentle snap of the strap we were on our way. The route we were taking was in hill country so Russ struggled to keep the tow strap taut as we went up and down hill and dale. We had noticed outbound that of the several little towns we passed through only Vienna had anything that resembled a service station. It was nearly 5 PM as our joined vehicles pulled onto the shoulder just in front of that business. Whether it was permanently closed or just presently closed we couldn't tell but either way they were not going to be any help to us. It was now getting dark. Should we unhook the car and leave it here or keep going? Russ wanted to continue to the Ford dealer in Jefferson City. I looked at his eyes and they were not too bugged out from continually trying to prevent my boat from crashing through his windshield, so I told him OK and promised to keep it under 50 miles per hour.

It was pitch black when we finally pulled into the dealership lot. As I was making the last turn to position Russ near the service department, I heard a slight "clunk" and I realized Russ was being left behind. I parked and walked back to find that the tow strap had worn through at the last possible moment. The strap had served its purpose. We pushed the car into a parking space and since they were closed, Russ dropped the keys in the after hour depository with instructions to repair whatever was necessary to get the car running as long as it cost under $300.

From there it was a 45 minute drive to the campground where we were going to spend the night. We pulled in, paid our fee, set up the tent, built a fire, popped a cold beer, fixed and ate a delicious supper of salad, T-bone steaks and baked potatoes. For dessert we had a second cold beer. We walked down to the river to view our objective in the dark, brooding moonlight, returned to the fire, drank one last beer, slipped into our sleeping bags and slept like babes until the sun awoke us on a clear, cold morning.

Since we were expecting a day filled with manly adventure, I thought it only right that we have a hearty breakfast: scrambled eggs, bacon, toast and coffee. Well, it was not real coffee, it was instant. I found an ancient jar of semi-coagulated instant coffee crystals in the spice cabinet at home (Janet and I don't usually drink coffee) and knowing that Russ and I would be wanting something warm to drink, I had thrown it in the box of food supplies. What I didn't know was that since college Russ had learned to take his morning coffee fairly seriously and he eyed me with some trepidation as I jabbed a knife into the jar attempting to break off two lumps to throw in the bottom of our coffee cups. After the boiling water was added and stirred, I took a sip from my cup and pronounced the taste and smell delightful. Russ, having something that slightly approximated his morning requirement, sipped appreciatively.

Down came the tent, we bagged all our equipment and loaded it in the boat, which was still in the back of the pickup. I drove the truck around to the boat ramp and backed about halfway down. We removed most of the equipment and placed it nearby on the river bank. I moved the two heavy trolling batteries onto the tailgate, where they would be easy to transfer into the boat once we had it in the water. We were preparing to slide the boat out of the truck and into the water when I decided that our job would be easier if I backed the truck down the ramp just a few more feet. I got behind the wheel and keeping Russ in clear view in my side mirror, I eased the truck on down. Russ signaled me to stop with a raised hand and at the instant I touched my foot to the brake, I heard a scraping sound. At first, I saw Russ seem to move forward and then leap wildly away from the boat ramp as the two batteries slid off the tailgate and crashed onto the concrete, cracking open and spraying acid everywhere. Russ had some splatters on the legs of his blue jeans (these would probably become holes after he got home and had them laundered) but the acid did not hit any bare skin. We unloaded the boat and since there was no reason to cry over spilt battery acid, I loaded the now empty hulks into my truck and headed to the local Wal-Mart that was about ten miles down the road. There I wheeled them in a shopping cart back to the automotive department, where I explained to the assistant manager that I needed two new batteries. He saw that the one battery was a new purchase and offered to make an exchange at no cost. I explained that I had no receipt and it had been purchased in a Wal-Mart fifty miles away. He said, "It's clear you have some bad luck this morning. I think we can do this little favor for you." Of course, I had to buy a replacement battery for the one I'd borrowed from my father-in-law but needless to say I was very happy. They put both batteries on their quick charger and in a short time I was on my way.

It was nearly 11 AM by the time we had everything squared away and had pushed off onto the river. Russ suggested we should motor the mile or so upstream to the dam so we could honestly claim we had traveled the entire route. Good idea. I turned the bow upstream and we began to putt along. With the speed control on #2 we were just staying even with the boat ramp. I cranked it up to #4—top speed. We began to creep towards our goal. After about twenty minutes we had made it around a bend and could just glimpse the dam about ¾ of a mile off. I expressed battery power/time concerns to Russ and we decided a glimpse would suffice. I turned the boat around and we started downstream.

The sun had been out during the morning but as the day progressed it began to cloud up. We moved downstream for about an hour and a half when we decided to pull over onto a gravel bar and have lunch. As we finished our sandwiches, I let Russ know about my plans for supper. The main course was going to be fried fish and considering that we hadn't had even a nibble so far, I thought it was a good idea to let him know so he wouldn't let down his efforts.

While we were on shore we also discussed our progress. About 1/5 of the way downriver we would pass under a state highway bridge so we considered this a good landmark to measure our progress by. I had brought along the highway map I had used previously to estimate the length of our journey and as we proceeded downstream, this map was ever more frequently consulted in a vain attempt to figure out where we were.

By late afternoon it was completely overcast and we knew that there'd be little light after sunset. Russ had succeeded in catching two fish and we began to seriously look for a campsite. We were aware when we scheduled the trip that this weekend was the start of deer hunting season. We had taken the precaution of bringing a plastic, hunter orange vest to put on whenever we wandered away from the river. Gun shots had been common all day and we began to think that a campsite on a gravel bar backed up to a steep bluff might prevent us from being awakened the next day by a bullet tearing through our tent. We had been traveling for quite a while on the side of the valley where the river was near the bluffs but as the sky continued to darken no suitable gravel bar appeared. Finally, as the distant views began to get fuzzy due to failing light, we spotted a rocky ledge at the foot of some cliffs ahead on the left. We pulled over and clambered up the slope about ten feet above the river to find a small area where a fire could be built and tent pitched. The whole area was slightly sloping to the river and one misstep in the night could cause a sleepy river man to end up floating downstream, but there was a nearby dead tree for firewood so we called it good enough.

The two fried fish, a hastily chopped head of cabbage, which when doused with salad dressing became slaw and various half eaten bags of chips and crackers was our sumptuous repast. It was heavily overcast and when it became fully dark we realized we could see the glow of three different communities reflected on the clouds. The road map was retrieved from the boat and we spent the next half hour trying to use these faint illuminations to triangulate our location. This failed due to our inability to differentiate between the glow of a small nearby village and the glow of a faraway city. A wire bread twist tie was retrieved from the cooking supplies and shaped into the bends and turns of the river on our map in an attempt to figure how far we had traveled but this too failed. We knew for certain that we had not passed under the highway bridge that was to mark our 1/5 progress and since our weekend was now half over we would not succeed in making the entire journey.

The cold set in hard after supper. We piled on any extra clothes and even though we did not have an excess of firewood we built up the fire. That mystery of a burning fire began to enter our hearts. The conversation moved from work, to politics, then onto the really important topics of life and God. Men sitting around a campfire will discuss things that they would never consider talking about anywhere else. There is a warm, private security to a campfire which is made more wonderful by a cold night. Cold weather forces you from time to time to turn your posterior towards the flame to prevent one side from freezing while the other side cooks. When you suddenly turn and face away from the fire you realize how separate your little camp is. The fire casts its gentle colors on the distant bluff, the shadows of the bare trees dance, a distant cow calls to its calf and the overcast sky is like a blanket pulled over your head. The real world is out there—far away. The voice (and silence) of your friend, the energy giving fire, this circle of warmth is a source of mystery. A mystery that is impossible to find anywhere but outdoors.

A cold fog had settled over the river during the night. The sky was light when we crawled out of the tent but it would be another thirty minutes before the sun itself would appear, from behind the distant river bluffs, as a faint, cloud-wrapped disk. We enjoyed a second breakfast filled with calories, cholesterol and instant coffee. We each took turns donning the bright vest for our morning pilgrimage into the woods to answer the real call of nature.

With camp struck we were back on the river with the day shaping up to be similar to yesterday—cloudy with morning temperatures in the thirties and afternoon highs in the forties. The weather may have not been wonderful but the river itself was. The Osage River is a series of long, deep pools, usually about a half a mile long or longer followed by a run through shallow gravel areas. These runs always afforded enough water to prevent dragging on the bottom but only if the correct route was chosen. As our float down the river continued our skill at reading these correct routes improved. Twice yesterday we literally "scraped by" using the two oars as poles to push us off the gravel. This day we had been on the river only an hour when we had to make a quick decision between a broad shallow area to the right of a small island and the fast deep current to the left. The latter choice included obstructions provide by several trees that had been undercut by the current and were now dragging their leafless branches in the stream. We chose the safe route to the right but were soon, in spite of some Herculean straining on our oar/poles, hopelessly aground on the gravel in about five inches of water. Russ started to move about as if planning to step into the water but I told him to sit tight while I slowly removed my shoes, socks and pants. When I had been packing at home I had chosen boxers instead of briefs for just this eventuality. I figured that I'd be more comfortable being seen by a passing boat in my blue boxers than in my tidy-whities (or as some in the younger generation say—tighty-whities). I pulled on my old canvas tennis shoes and by just stepping out of the boat it nearly floated free. Some minor pulling on the front bow rope and we were soon on our way again.

I should mention that my concern about being seen in my underwear by a passing boat was unwarranted. After leaving the immediate environs of the dam, a popular fishing place due to the turbidity caused by the outwash of the turbines, we proceeded downriver entirely alone. Once we saw a farmer on a tractor in his field and twice a pickup truck driving down a nearby gravel road but on the river itself we were alone. This made it very easy to imagine we were traveling a river, this section at least, that had changed very little in the last one thousand years.

Most of the trees had lost their leaves by now. The river had a scattering of floating, narrow, willow leaves mixed with an occasional big oak leaf. Due to the fallen leaves, the rusty-green cedar trees on the hillside were now prominent. The now open hills were easily inspected for deer, turkey, squirrels, etc. in a way that would have been impossible just a few weeks earlier, when all was obscured by multi-hued green foliage. As one looked downriver, the mottled, bleached trunks of the sycamore trees stood like signposts marking the river's course. The most dramatic component of the view has to be the magnificent bluffs. They are white and beige, horizontal strata of limestone and dolomite, streaked with vertical charcoal colored stains that come from the weathering of included minerals. Most places they soar more than 100 feet above the river. Above and behind the bluffs are steep sided valleys and ravines that lead up to the thin ridges that separate one drainage basin from the next. In this part of the country, the older state highways run these ridges and from those high vantage points the valleys beckon.

The beauty of much of America, in my opinion, is hills and valleys. I have a friend that is an avid outdoorsman. Once I was talking to him about how many people, when talking about the beauty of nature, dismiss their homegrown variety. They begin to talk about the drama of the ocean, desert or mountains and on vacations return again and again to these places. They become displaced ocean-people or wannabe mountain-people. His response was that visiting the ocean was nice but all you could really do was stand on the edge and look out. The mountains of the West are beautiful but so immense that they appear impassible. But our hills and valleys call to you to come and see what is on the other side, call to you to tromp up and down hill and holler. I had to agree with him but said if we aren't ocean-people or mountain-people then we must be hill-people.

Hill-people is slightly more politically correct than the more familiar term, hillbillies. Hill-people are simple folk, who live a close to self-sufficient lifestyle, removed or remote from the modern world. A love of the simple life and being close to nature keeps them content. Some hippy types tried it for a few years but most returned to the real world. Genuine hill-people are very rare. I can think of only one family I've ever known and that was years ago. They lived at the bottom of a hill near the Gravois River in the Ozarks. By the mid-1960s just the old Ma and Pa were still there, all their children had grown up and moved away. There were still kids running around but they were the offspring of the many goats surrounding their little two room house. The goats lived in the many junk cars scattered up the hill. A very neat, big garden was located near the river. My family used to stop and collect watercress from the cold, clear water near a low-water concrete bridge just across from their house. My dad was the type who often struck up conversations with strangers and I guess over the years he had become familiar with the old couple. The old man was always in bib overalls and she was a small, old woman in a dress like my grandmother wore in pictures from the 1930s.

They were still living with no electricity. They did have running water, in the yard at least. A capped spring near their house always shot water about three feet high before it ran into a storage barrel and then down to the river. Those old folks were real hill-people—hillbillies in the truest, simplest sense of the word.

Today as you drive Ozark roads you'll see a different country lifestyle. These folks would be what my parents would have called white trash. They live in a rundown house surrounded by three sleeping dogs in the yard, two cars, two pickups, four junk motorcycles, a broken down RV, a huge abandoned satellite dish and two boats. These folks have an innate need to be close to nature but certainly don't want to miss out on the modern obsession with accumulating "stuff".

While Russ and I were floating we discussed these topics. We agreed that our motivation for being on the Osage River was to find contentment in a simple life close to nature. But there could be no denying with all this mismatched, broken down, fishing and camping equipment, not to mention the whole car towing escapade, that it might be proper if we called ourselves the White Trash River Boys.

As the day progressed and no highway bridge appeared we began to think of our float not as something to accomplish but something to experience. The sound of a wave lapping the side of the aluminum boat, a red tailed hawk circling above, the sweet crunch of peanuts and M&M's, the cold but soft, fresh air, the hollow plop of a perfectly cast lure all combined with a hundred different moments to make the afternoon one of quiet joy.

At about three in the afternoon we rounded a bend and saw the copper dome of a county courthouse on a distant bluff—Tuscumbia, the county seat of Maries County, the place with the long awaited highway bridge. The bridge came into view after we skirted around a gravel dredging barge. Ahead on the left was a Department of Conservation boat ramp. As Russ tied up the boat, I walked up into town in search of a pay phone. Before I left home for this adventure, the last thing I said to my wife after I kissed her goodbye was, "Since we really don't know what we're doing, would you please be at home by the phone Sunday afternoon? We may need to call you for help."

In about an hour and a half Janet appeared. Russ stayed with the boat and equipment while she drove me back to my truck at the campground where we started. When we returned we loaded the boat in the back of my truck and stacked all my gear inside it. We loaded Russ' stuff in Janet's car so she could drive him back to Jeff City to check on his invalid car.

When we finished this frantic activity, Russ and I walked to the edge of the river for one last look. Janet took our picture to record this moment for history. Russ and I both mumbled something about how great a weekend this had been and walked towards the car. We shook hands. Russ opened the door, sat down and pulled it shut. At that moment we both must have had the same idea, because as I stepped forward preparing to speak, he rolled down the window and said, "We should meet here next year and continue our journey." I said, "Sounds great," and raised one hand in a motionless wave as they drove off.

CHAPTER TWO

Six on the River

My friend Ralf and I pulled up to the boat ramp in Tuscumbia on a clear, warm mid-October Friday afternoon.   Like last year, I had an aluminum rowboat sticking out of the back of my slightly rusted Ford pickup.   Remembering last year's disaster with the batteries, I had carefully stowed them where they could not slide out.   It was right at 3 PM but we were the last to arrive.

About a month ago, I had called Russ to make plans to return to the Osage River for what we hoped would become an annual event. We laid out the general plan to float the next section of river, Tuscumbia to St. Thomas. Less than a week later he called back. It seems that last Christmas when visiting with his brothers they had been intrigued by his tale of our adventure. He was now calling to see if I would be receptive to the notion of expanding our outing to include them. I knew them both to be avid outdoorsmen and I was flattered to think that our little float would appeal to them. I believed that their fishing skills would be well appreciated and I knew them both to be friendly and fun loving personalities. I mentioned that my former college roommate, Dan had also expressed interest. That made five. Russ was sure his brothers, Bob and Mike could find two boats, so if we wanted to ask one more that would make two per boat. That's how my friend Ralf got the nod.

I pulled around and saw that the boat ramp was clear so I backed down. At the bottom were Russ and Dan both fishing from the end of the ramp. Bob and Mike were fiddling with an old gas motor on the back of one of the two boats. Ralf and I stepped out and he was introduced to everyone. I had not seen Bob for several years and had the common experience of seeing a friend and thinking how much he resembles his father. I kept that thought to myself and thankfully he did too, although he did mention that I had hair the last time he saw me.

Russ comes from a large family and I know his brothers well. My dad and their father were crappie fishing and quail hunting partners. Although we were in grade and high school together, Russ and I had not become close friends until college. His brother Bob and I had been close since childhood. We were bike riding, hunting, swimming, camping buddies. He was two years ahead of me in school but even in high school he always invited me to tag along. That's a pretty big deal when you're a freshman and your friend is a junior. Mike, the youngest of the three, was cut from the same cloth. And to let you know, Dan, my college roommate, is their cousin. That's proof that I grew up in a small town.

It only took a couple of minutes to get my boat in the water and loaded. Just before we started, a mouse, which had set up housekeeping under one of the enclosed boat seats, ran out and began to climb over our camping gear. With a little encouragement from one of the paddles he leaped over the side and dove into the river. He quickly realized he was swimming the wrong way and with steady strokes made a small arc and headed for shore. A moment later he was on the bank and hurried across the rocks to the tangle of roots of a nearby tree. I took that to be a good omen. If he would have appeared when we were in the middle of the river I'm sure he would have caused considerable excitement and he may not have survived. Now that our uninvited guest had scurried off we pushed the boats into the stream, Ralf with me, Dan in the front of Mike's boat and Russ with Bob.

Last year Russ and I had floated in early November. Due to two fairly nippy nights and the concern about being out during deer season, this year we had moved the float to the third weekend in October. We expected the weather to be a bit milder and since Bob and Mike were deer hunters the change suited them. The rescheduling had worked out well. It was an absolutely gorgeous day. Clear air, deep blue sky punctuated by a few scattered fluffy clouds, temperature in the mid-sixties. We floated past a gravel bar on our right and turned the boat into the main current of the river.

As I mentioned, we were in my aluminum rowboat powered by my battery powered trolling motor—the same outfit I had used last year. It was piled high with camping and fishing equipment. My rowboat has a typical pointed bow, fairly stable but a bit tippy, especially in the front. The type of boat most familiar to river floaters, in this part of the country, would be aluminum canoes. They are tippy every-which-way. We were trailing a few yards behind the other two boats and that gave us a chance to assess our fellow adventurers. Dan was in the front of Mike's boat. It was a small aluminum jon boat with a flaking blue stripe painted on the side. Jon boats have a square bow and stern with a flat bottom. Their shallow draft and stability make them ideal craft for river floating. Some of the natural stability of Mike's boat was being compromised because they were so loaded down with coolers, tents, fishing equipment, etc. there was barely three inches between the water level and the top of the gunwale. The design of the boat might mean they would not tip over but it didn't take much imagination to see them foundered. On the back of his boat, he had a dinky little battery powered trolling motor and a truly ancient outboard motor. His seats were some swivel bar stools with the legs cut off mounted on plywood panels secured to the boat with woodworking clamps. Bob's boat was also a jon boat just a fuzz bigger than Mike's. It was loaded with the same amount of gear as Mike's boat but since it was slightly larger and didn't have an outboard motor it was not so low in the water. One interesting feature of both boats was that jumbled everywhere were five gallon plastic buckets. They had determined that these buckets with snap on lids make excellent waterproof storage bins. That was true but since they were round and slippery, they refused to stay put in the boat and tended to slide and roll about adding to the general disheveled appearance. Looking over our entourage I decided that last year's White Trash River Boys designation was appropriate.

The trip began by passing under the curved-top, steel highway bridge at Route 52. This was the couldn't-be-missed landmark Russ and I had fruitlessly looked for last year. Soon we rounded a bend and left all signs of civilization behind. That characteristic of this river was one of the biggest surprises of our float last year—the fact that frequently one lost all indications of the modern world. The sky, the birds, the bluffs, the trees, the gravel bars, the river itself, all appeared as God had made them. Our choosing to float several weeks earlier than last year provided another advantage other than the mild weather. The trees this week were in their full glory. Most of the oaks still had their varying shades of rusty leaves. The sycamores were busy filling the river with their large, flat, floating leaves and the willow's golden leaves spun wildly as they descended into our boats.

I never considered myself much of a fisherman. Last year, if Russ had not pulled two fish from the river, supper the second night would have been skimpy. I had high expectations of a bountiful fried fish supper this year because of Mike and Bob being along. I was pleased to see everyone moving slowing down the river, seriously working downed logs and sunken driftwood piles for bass. Ralf in my boat quickly got his gear out and joined in. I had my pole rigged with a small plastic grub but for the most part I simply steered the boat. One thing that I remembered about last year was that after about one hour of being on the river, I could feel a physiological transformation begin to take place and so I felt no need to busy myself with fishing.

If you joined us on the river, I think you would have a similar experience. The days before the float, you are busy shopping, packing, inventorying and gathering food, drinks and gear. The morning of the expedition is hectic with final packing and loading. An hour or more drive gets you to the river, then more unloading and loading. Finally, you are on the river and you look around and say to yourself, "This is great!" You point out some beautiful natural scene to your boat mate. You rig up your fishing pole. You converse with your boat mate. You rearrange some inconvenient items in the boat. You say a few more brief words. Then you become silent. Slowly you begin to realize that you are really here, within the sanctuary of nature. Now begins the transformation. All those days of action begin to melt into inaction. Layers of the modern world seem to peel off. You suddenly notice the fresh crispness of the air. You say half aloud, "My, the sky is blue!" The low sunlight shimmering on the water is indescribable. You watch the wind surge through the trees on a nearby hill. A single laugh floats back from a boat ahead. Inside you become quiet, relaxed. You become the person you want to be.

With my hand on the tiller we drifted along behind the others. Occasionally, a nearly inaudible hoot carried across the water as someone lifted a flickering fish. We spent a couple of hours trailing the others. As the sun began to near the horizon, Ralf and I decided to pull ahead of the others to see if we could spot a suitable gravel bar for our campsite. As the evening light began to take on a golden autumn glow, we rounded a bend and spotted a gravel point ahead where the river during higher water would have split around an island. We pulled in and found that just above the point was a flat gravel bar with plenty of driftwood for a fire. As the other two boats came in one by one, the consensus was that this location would do quite well.

When I invited everyone on the float, I told them I would buy all the food for the meals. They only needed to bring the snacks and beverages they would want for themselves. Last year Russ and I had enjoyed a T-bone steak supper the first night and fried fish the second. That seemed like a good menu so I had planned to stick with it. With everyone working, within a few minutes scattered driftwood on the gravel bar had been accumulated into the largest pile of firewood I had ever seen at a campsite. Mike quickly kindled a fire just to one side of the wood pile and I began to move food supplies about looking for the steaks, potatoes and beans that would be tonight's repast. The others were setting up tents.

As the last light faded, coolers and five gallon buckets were brought near the fire. The seat in the front of my boat was a folding chair and it was retrieved and placed near the other more improvised seats. Before dinner there was time for a beer and a general discussion of what had been seen, caught or heard while we were separated on the river. Another beer was opened while supper was cooking. Since it was quite dark at this point, eating was a bit difficult. No one owned a lantern and while each of us had a flashlight, it was a challenge to balance a large Styrofoam plate on your lap, cut off a bite of steak without cutting all the way through to your knee, hold your flashlight so you could see to use your fork and still not upset the whole arrangement as you reached for your beer. Somehow we managed and within a short time there were contented moans and groans as we each in turn rose and tossed our now bare T-bone into the fire. Since I had cooked, I excused myself as water was heated to wash the dishes.

It certainly is a joy to be standing around a campfire with friends in October but it may be a greater pleasure to walk 50 yards away and enjoy the clear cool night alone. This night a quarter moon was high in the sky providing enough illumination to see that a little fog was beginning to snake along the river but high overhead the stars were shining clearly. At this early nighttime hour the air was still and cool. By morning we would be well dampened with dew. The bare trunks and branches of the sycamores along the riverbank glowed in the soft moonlight like spirits of departed friends. The river seemed dark and dangerous except very near the shore where it shimmered in the moonlight. Downriver a large bird—an owl?—flapped heavily across to the opposite bank. Somewhere a fish slapped the water. My nature watching was interrupted by laughter at the fire. I turned to watch the camaraderie encircling the fire. Most figures were in silhouette, some seated, some standing. The glowing, relaxed features of the men who faced my direction and the hallowed glow surrounding those whose backs were to me, made the night air seem suddenly cold. I briskly walked back to rejoin the circle.

Male bonding is the modern phrase for men spending time together. It's an overused, trite expression. It seems to me that modern men rarely make time for being with other men. Others might argue that point. What about work? What about soft ball teams, hunting, golf, volunteering with a fraternal group? I respond that all those activities are activities, they involve doing something. Six men being together, doing nothing but talking (well, maybe also a little drinking) around a campfire for 6-8 hours is really being together. Sure, the conversation begins with the stuff men are accused of always talking about but near midnight it is common for the conversation to move to the beauty of the stars, the meaningfulness of being a father, the understanding of freedom or the search for God. Did a brown bottle being passed from hand to hand have something to do with this introspection? No doubt. Willingness to sneak a fart in church aside, men are a bundle of inhibitions and it usually takes darkness, time, friendship and sometimes, yes, peach brandy to get them to speak from the heart.

I made it just past midnight that night. I said my good nights and moved through the darkness to the tent. A few unzips and zips later, I was in my sleeping bag and soon drifted to sleep listening to the quiet murmur of the voices of the more hardy souls still at the fire. Due to the late night we weren't early risers. The sound of twigs being snapped to bring the fire back to life awoke me at seven and I chose not to climb out of my warm bed until eight. Like last year, I had thrown a half empty jar of instant coffee crystals into the food box. So I was pleasantly surprised as I approached the fire. Mike was pouring Ralf a cup of coffee from a small aluminum percolator. He had just removed it from being balanced on two logs in the fire. I rooted around in the cookware and found a cup for myself. Mike filled my cup. Fresh perked coffee! In the cold morning air a generous steam cloud rose from the cup. I never smelled better coffee. I never tasted better coffee.

When I first climbed out of the tent everything on the gravel bar was cold and damp but now, just a few moments later, the sun was coming up from behind the bluff. Within minutes the delicious coffee and the direct sunshine had transformed the morning with its clear, strong warmth. Standing around a morning campfire visiting and drinking coffee compares favorably with standing around a nighttime campfire visiting and drinking beer. After a while, I fried some bacon and scrambled some eggs. Toast was made over the hot coals. We didn't seem to be in any hurry to leave our bright camp. We enjoyed more coffee and let the sun dry the dew off the tents.

Finally we loaded up and pushed off onto the river. I looked at my watch. It was just a few minutes past ten o'clock.

Our second day on the river was a repeat of the first. Good weather, a beautiful river and reasonably good fishing. One small point of concern did begin to surface in my own mind. We were moving downriver more slowly than expected. Last year Russ and I had pressed on fairly directly because we were under the mistaken impression we were going to travel a large section of this river in one weekend. When planning this year's float, I knew how far we had gotten, added some extra distance for the time we had lost replacing our broken batteries and had decided we could easily float from Tuscumbia to St. Thomas. What I hadn't factored-in was the seriousness these guys would place on catching our supper. They carefully worked each downed tree and backwater.

Bob had brought along a county map that was substantially better than last year's highway map. By mid-afternoon after some in depth analysis of the map by all six of us, coupled with some haggling over the direction of true north, it was clear that we could not make it to St. Thomas tomorrow without a major change in our rate of progress. The consensus was that we were having too good of a time to start hurrying up. More consultation of the map indicated that there was a boat ramp/campground at Tavern Creek just about the right distance to allow us another night on the river and an early Sunday arrival.

Reinvigorated by a braunschweiger with spicy mustard sandwich and a new plan we returned to the river to enjoy the rest of the daylight. Just after sunset another appealing gravel bar appeared and we pulled in. Enough fish had been caught for a hearty supper and we found ourselves enjoying another evening together. A cold night, a warm breakfast and we were on the river again. By mid-morning we pulled into Tavern Creek.

The plan made the night before was that Ralf and I would hitchhike back to Tuscumbia. We hoped to find some campers at Tavern Creek who we could approach with our request for a ride. As we walked up the boat ramp we were disappointed to find the campground empty. The map was again consulted. It was about a four mile hike up a gravel road to the main highway. Ralf was game, so we tied up my boat, the others shoved off to do more fishing and we took off.

About a mile up the road we came to a farmer spending his Sunday morning feeding six pigs in a tumbled down feedlot. He was shaking corn from a five gallon bucket into a trough as we walked by. We called out a good morning but kept walking up the road. He seemed busy and I was too shy to disturb him. About fifteen minutes later he caught up with us in his old pickup. I flagged him down. He was going the opposite way from Tuscumbia but he was happy to give us a ride to the main road. We climbed in the cab and in a few minutes were dropped off at the main highway. After a sincere thank you, we began walking along the shoulder of the highway. Here, the highway follows a bluff along the river and we could look between the bare trees down 200 feet to the winding river below. Yesterday, we had enjoyed the same view on the river looking up but now it was even more beautiful looking the other direction. We walked about a mile and came to a small house where three people were just piling into a cab of an old pickup with a flat bed on the back. I called out that we where needing a ride to Tuscumbia, would they consider giving us a lift? The driver said that they were going right by there and told us to climb on the back.

We sort of crouched/sat on the wooden truck bed between parts of a disemboweled automatic transmission. We hung onto whatever we could find as the truck weaved and turned its way up and down hills on the 20 minute ride. I could look through the truck's rear window and see the speedometer. He never got us over 60 miles per hour but from where Ralf and I sat it felt more like 100. It was like being on a roller coaster without the metal safety bar to cling to. We crossed the steel bridge where we had begun our journey and at a highway intersection about a half mile north of town, they dropped us off. Three hours after we left, we drove back into the parking lot at Tavern Creek.

It was early afternoon when I backed down the boat ramp. As we emptied the boat so we could lift it onto the truck, the others who were fishing nearby came over to help. We had Bob's truck at Tuscumbia and Russ' car at St. Thomas so it took some discussion to plan how we were going to shuttle everyone to the proper location. Before we went our separate ways, Russ pulled out his camera and balanced it on the tailgate of my truck. Setting the timer he rushed back to join the group photo. Broad smiles and firm handshakes were made all around. Bob climbed in with Ralf and me and we drove up the gravel road we had just walked a few hours earlier. After dropping Bob at the parking lot in Tuscumbia, I circled the truck and we headed for home. Ahead, I could just glimpse the curved top of the highway bridge that had become such a landmark for us on this trip. Ralf made some comment about how nice the weather had been. I agreed, and thought to myself, the White Trash River Boys have really come up with something good here!

CHAPTER THREE

White Trash River Cooking

I've said much about the joys of spending time in nature and much about the joys of manly companionship but I would not be complete in describing our annual outings without a few detailed words about food. From the very beginning I strived to make our mealtimes an important part of our experiences. This was done in the beginning to prove that while we were out spiritually feeding on the bountiful palette of the natural world our physical needs would not be met by consuming a plate of hot dogs and potato chips.

For all the years we have been on the river, we've had a traditional menu—the first night steaks, the second night fish. And as the years progressed, I will admit to some streamlining of the cooking process. I used to enjoy chopping onions and dicing bacon while sitting on a log near the campfire but now I do almost all the prep work in my kitchen at home. Here's the menu we enjoy every year.

First night—Grilled rib steaks, baked potato with butter and sour cream, camp beans and pickled okra as a before dinner appetizer.

First breakfast—Breakfast burritos.

Second night—Fried or blackened fish, dirty rice, slaw and cornbread with butter and honey.

Second breakfast—Fried eggs, fried venison sausage, cinnamon-raisin toast with butter.

Lunches—Braunschweiger or summer sausage sandwiches on wheat rolls or bagels. Swiss cheese and hot mustard make the sandwiches complete. Something crunchy, like corn chips or snack mix, is also provided.

Of course some special treats always seem to appear—Donna's chocolate chip cookies, venison sausage snacks, White Trash Licker, simple trail mix, Snickers candy bars, peach brandy, etc.

Camp Cooking Advice

I cook using a grill that has folding legs that holds the grill about 12" off the ground. We routinely have a large fire going but I don't use it for my cooking. I set up my grill a convenient distance from the main fire and using a long handled, square shovel I transport hot coals and place them on the ground under the grill. This has several advantages; you can regulate how hot your fire is by adding/removing coals, the stable grill creates a good level surface for your skillet or pot and if the weather is a bit warm it keeps you from becoming overheated working around a large fire. If you are in a hurry to get something boiling or frying, some dry twigs on the coals will flame up heating a pot or skillet faster than the coals alone.

I use a heavy cast iron 13" skillet for all my frying. I have a cast iron pot with lid (8 quarts) for all my other cooking. You can see that most of my recipes use things like bacon and butter. Old fashioned cast iron works very well with this type of old fashioned cooking. We don't count fat, calories or carbs when we are on the river. I would not like to eat this type of food everyday but if you are outdoors all day long and it is cool weather, you and your comrades will look forward to each meal.

As a serving note, we use large disposal foam trays as plates. After supper they burn right up with little environmental impact. We use real forks and steak knives; they require washing after each meal but are worth it. A tiny bottle of liquid soap and a scouring pad make washing the dishes in the cook pot easy enough. A quick wipe with an old towel and everything is ready for tomorrow.

Here are the recipes. These recipes will serve six men.

Grilled Rib Steaks

6 rib steaks
2 oz. whiskey
2 oz. water

2 oz. olive oil
2 oz. Italian salad dressing
A hearty shake of garlic powder
A less hearty shake of black pepper

Stop by the local meat counter 4-6 days before you hit the river. Tell the butcher that every year you buy six of the nicest rib steaks you can find to cook for your boys on the river. Tell him you want them cut an inch thick. I guarantee you he will come back with the best steaks he has. A day or so before leaving, mix together in a shallow glass pan the six non-steak ingredients listed above. Dredge the steaks in this marinade and make sure they are well covered. Remove steaks from pan and slip them into a couple of zip-top plastic bags. Drizzle any remaining marinade on steaks. Put in refrigerator. Turn occasionally. When on the river, I cook the steaks on the grill directly over hot coals. You can judge the temperature of the coals by holding your hand about four inches over the grill and counting the number of seconds you can keep your hand in place. "One second, two seconds, yikes!" is about right. I put the steaks on the grill, cook, flip once, tell the guys to get their plates ready and then let them choose when to remove the steak of their choice—that way everyone gets a steak the way he wants it.

Baked Potatoes

In case you missed out on basic Boy Scout training, this is as simple as you can get. Choose six large potatoes, scrub, cut off any surface defects, stab with a fork and wrap in aluminum foil. Rake some hot coals to one side and bury the potatoes in coals. They usually take only about 20 minutes. Check for doneness by jabbing with a fork or knife. If they pass that test, as you remove them from the coals, with a gloved hand squeeze each to confirm that it is soft all the way through. Don't be misled and over bake them. If they are over baked, a hard, outer crust will form. Don't forget to pack the salt and pepper and in my opinion butter and sour cream are essential.

Camp Beans

One 15 oz. can each, white beans, red beans and black beans
One medium sized onion
1/2 pound bacon diced
BBQ sauce
Heaping tablespoon brown sugar
Squirt of hot mustard

In a sauce pan over the fire fry the bacon and onion together. Drain beans and dump into sauce pan. Glug in some BBQ sauce, add the brown sugar and mustard. Heat through.

Breakfast Burritos

12 large flour tortillas
1 pound sliced county cured ham
10 fresh eggs
1/2 medium onion diced
1/2 green pepper diced
1/2 pound cubed cheddar cheese
Salsa
Maybe some cooking oil

Remove fat, skin and bone from ham. Dice ham. Throw several big pieces of fat in skillet and fry up. If skillet is still not well coated with grease add a small splash of cooking oil. Fry the ham. At some point remove and discard the fat. When ham is done remove skillet from fire and break in the 10 eggs. The skillet is probably hot enough at this point that the eggs will cook off the fire. When the eggs are pretty well done (cooked scrambled style) throw in the cheese and return to the fire to heat through. I let each man choose whether to use any salsa because some in our group believe that any meal before 11 AM is too early for salsa. If you have leftover sour cream from last night's baked potatoes, some might like a dab. Just before serving remove skillet from grill and allow each man to heat his tortilla on the grill before making and rolling up a burrito.

Fried Fish

Boneless, skinless, fish fillets
Cooking oil
1/2 stick butter

Fried Fish Coating

1 cup corn meal
1 cup flour
1/4 cup sugar
1/3 cup dry powdered milk
2 teaspoon baking powder
1 teaspoon Cajun seasoning
1/2 teaspoon salt

Mix all the ingredients for the Fried Fish Coating. When I fry fish at the river the fillets are very fresh and recently washed. If you are frying fish at home you might want to soak the fillets briefly in beer or milk so they are damp enough for the dry coating to stick. I usually spread out some aluminum foil, sprinkle some coating across the foil, lay out the fillets and dump more coating on top. I like to work the coating in with my fingers. Do this with only one hand so the other is kept clean. I make sure I have all the fillets prepped before I start frying. Put the skillet on the grill with about ½ inch oil in it. Throw in the ½ stick butter. I use a fairly hot fire under the skillet (1,2,3 yikes!) Keep a close eye on the skillet, the secret here is having the right temperature.

Smoking oil is too hot. When I suspect the heat is about right I'll throw in one small piece. If it starts frying very aggressively more of the fillets can go in. Don't crowd them in the skillet. Turn only once. I usually bring along several aluminum, throw-away pie pans. As the fillets come out of the skillet they can go into the pie pans and be kept warm near the fire until all the fish have been fried.

Blackened Fish Fillets
Boneless, skinless fish fillets
One or more sticks butter
Blackened fish seasoning

Every other year we have blackened fish instead of fried. Don't try this recipe in your kitchen—a tremendous amount of smoke is created. (I have first hand experience on that point!) Melt the butter in a pie pan. Dredge each fillet through the butter. Sprinkle both sides with blackening seasoning. I suggest you be conservative with the seasoning, fresh fish have a delicate flavor that is easily overpowered. Prep all the fillets before you begin blackening. Remove a large quantity of hot coals from the fire. Place a clean, dry, cast iron skillet directly on the coals. Don't be afraid to let the skillet get hot—it may take on an almost whitish sheen. Add the fillets in the skillet in a single layer. Each fillet will take only a short time on each side. Turn once. If you are doing more than two batches of fish you might have to add more coals because the weight of the skillet sitting directly on the coals will begin to put them out.

Dirty Rice

1½ cups rice
1/2 pound of bacon diced
1/2 pound of pork sausage, polish sausage or andouille sausage
One onion chopped
One green pepper chopped
15 oz. can of diced canned tomatoes
15 oz. jar of salsa (or whatever is left over from the breakfast burritos)

Cook the rice per the package directions. It is not difficult to cook rice over a campfire but to make my life easier; I do this step at home. At the campfire, I use my cast iron cook pot to fry the bacon and sausage. When it is about ¾ done add in the onion and green pepper. When all this is done if it all seems a little to greasy, you can spoon out some of the excess. Then add in the cooked rice, canned tomatoes and salsa. Stir together and set aside near the fire to keep warm while you are fixing the fish. The longer it sets the better it gets.

Cole Slaw

One medium head of cabbage
1 cup white vinegar
1 cup diced onion
3/4 cup salad oil
2/3 cup sugar
1 tablespoon prepared mustard
1 teaspoon celery seeds

If you make this up two or three days before going to the river it will be at its peak of flavor. I use a food processor to slice the cabbage thin. Also thin slice the onion. I put all the other ingredients in a sauce pan and heat slowly, stirring to dissolve the sugar. When it just begins to boil, I throw in the onion and remove it from the burner. I let the mixture cool for about 20 minutes. With the sliced cabbage in a very large bowl I pour in part of the liquid mixture, stopping to toss the liquid over the cabbage. It should just wilt the cabbage very slightly. If the liquid is too hot let it cool some more before adding the rest and tossing. This slaw can be stored up to a week in the refrigerator. For the first several days, stir twice a day to distribute the excess liquid over the cabbage. This is Grandma's recipe and in addition to taking it to the river, I frequently take it to family gatherings. It's easy to make, it is delicious and everyone thinks of Grandma when eating it.

Corn Bread

3/4 cup toasted corn meal

(Toasted corn meal is better than regular but is a bit difficult to find. If necessary, you can substitute regular or you can first lightly toast the corn meal on a shallow pan in the oven.)

1¼ cup flour

1/4 cup sugar

4 teaspoons baking powder

1/2 teaspoon salt

1 cup milk

1/4 cup shortening

One egg

With the proper equipment this can be baked over the fire but I don't intend to slave over the campfire so I cheat and bake it the night before we leave. Heat the oven to 425 degrees. Grease a 12 inch cast iron skillet. Mix all the dry ingredients together in a bowl then add all the wet ingredients. Stir together for about one minute and pour into skillet. Bake 20-25 minutes or until a toothpick stuck in the middle comes out clean. After cooling, I wrap it in a double layer of aluminum foil. At the river, reheat it by placing it on some coals and piling a few more on top. I like honey with my corn bread, so I take some in a glass jar. If it is very cold, the honey should be left near the fire for a while. That way it is not too stiff to use on the warm cornbread.

Venison Sausage, Fried Eggs
and Raisin Cinnamon Toast

This is just a simple fried breakfast so no
recipe is necessary. Of course, if you have no
venison sausage you can use pork. I put a little oil
in the skillet because there is not much fat in deer
sausage. After the sausage is done, move it to a
pie pan to be kept warm. Add more oil to the
skillet and return the skillet to the fire. When I
think the oil is hot enough I remove the skillet and
break all 12 eggs into the hot oil then I return the
skillet to the fire. When the eggs are nearly done,
you can again remove the skillet from the fire.
The residual heat in the skillet will finish the job.
While that is happening it only takes a couple
minutes for some of the guys to toast the bread
slices on the grill and butter them. And yeah,
toasted over a campfire, the raisin cinnamon toast
is way better than plain toast.

Donna's Chocolate Chip Cookies

This is the only recipe I don't prepare
myself. Many years ago, Gene's wife sent some
cookies along with him. The next year Donna
made them but he forgot and left them at home.
That was the last time he did that!

2/3 cup butter
2/3 cup butter flavored solid shortening

3/4 cup white sugar
3/4 cup brown sugar, packed
2 eggs
2 tsp. real vanilla extract
3 cups flour
1 tsp. baking soda
1 tsp. salt
1 pkg. (3½ ounce) instant vanilla pudding mix
1 pkg. (12 ounce) semi-sweet chocolate chips
1/2 cup baking raisins
1/2 cup shredded coconut

With a mixer, beat the butter and shortening together until fluffy. Add both sugars, beat until well blended. Beat in eggs and vanilla. Set aside. In a separate bowl mix together flour, soda, salt and pudding mix. Gradually add to the beaten mixture, stirring well. Stir in chocolate chips, coconut and raisins. Drop by heaping tablespoons onto ungreased cookie sheet. Bake at 350 for 14-18 minutes. Yield 4 dozen.

Donna's tips—Less mixing with the electric mixer will make softer, fluffier cookies. The best method is to mix by hand. Take the cookies out when they just barely look done. They will firm up after they cool completely. Doing this will make a softer, chewier cookie.

Simple Trail Mix

One part raisins
One part peanuts
One part plain M&Ms

Dump into a zipper bag and enjoy.

White Trash Licker

In an empty liquor bottle mix;
Two parts unflavored cheap brandy,
One part Amaretto liqueur

Take a piece of duct tape and cover the original bottle label and write W.T. Licker on the duct tape. This is a potent after dinner drink so no gulping.

Camp Coffee

Actually there is one other important item besides Donna's cookies on the menu that I take no part in preparing. That is the fresh brewed coffee we have every morning. I do not drink coffee as part of a daily routine. I expect that I drink about 10 cups a year. Of our bunch, I'm at one end of the spectrum and Russ is at the other, averaging I suspect about three cups a day. I am certain if you were to ask any of the six of us, we would say that the best coffee we have during the year is what Mike makes over that campfire in his beat-up little aluminum percolator. Each morning on the river he makes three full pots. Years ago, in a thrift store I found a nice stainless steel percolator much larger than the one he has and I bought it for him as a gift. I never gave it to him. You can't improve on perfection. I once asked him for his recipe. He said use Folgers coffee, water out of a plastic jug, have a smoky fire, let it perk until the color looks about right then serve it on a cold morning on a river bank to good friends. I'm sure if you add the last two ingredients to all the recipes I've written you'll create a memorable feast.

CHAPTER FOUR

"Wake Up, the Boats Are Gone!"

For three or four years we proceeded section by section down the Osage River. Every year we followed the same basic plan. Thursday afternoon we would drop Russ' car at this year's take-out boat ramp. We would then proceed to this year's starting point—the place where we had taken-out last year. After loading all the equipment in the boats, we then made a short float to our Thursday night campsite on a gravel bar. We would enjoy a supper of rib steaks with baked potatoes, a nice night spent on the gravel bar followed by breakfast burritos and Mike's fresh brewed coffee in the morning. Friday was spent floating, fishing and snacking on the river. A second gravel bar was chosen for a camp where we repeated last night's festivities except the supper was of fresh caught fish. The second morning, we enjoyed a hearty eggs and sausage breakfast with more coffee followed by the last few relaxing hours on the river. Usually we were off the river and on our way home by 3 PM Saturday. During those years the membership of our little corps had changed a bit. Russ and I, as founding members of our expedition, had not missed a year. His two brothers, Bob and Mike, had been equally faithful. Several years back my brother, Paul, joined us. This year we had a new participant, my neighbor Gene. Gene is about the same age as the rest of us. He owns a landscaping business and is an avid hunter. Like the rest of us he grew up on a farm so he seemed to instantly fit right in.

This year's float was the final section of the Osage just above where it joins the Missouri River. My father-in-law had warned me that this section of the river included an abandoned lock and dam that we would have to portage around. There was no indication of its location on the small county map we had, so as we launched, I warned everyone to be alert. If a low structure across the river was seen, pull to the right bank, away from the lock. The lock is a steep chute where all the water roars through when the river is low.

I had Russ in the front of my boat, Paul was with Bob and Gene was in Mike's boat. We began to fish, float and get in the spirit of the journey. After several hours Russ and I were trailing well behind the others and we were having some luck catching some keeper sized fish. With the light beginning to fade, I was pleased when we rounded a bend and saw that the other two boats had pulled over and they were beginning to make camp.

After all the tents were up, the evening firewood gathered and the coolers and boxes unloaded from the boats, everyone popped a beer and we gathered around the fire. At that point Bob and Mike began to discuss that due to a shifting wind; the location chosen for the fire was no longer convenient. The general topography of the gravel bar, the location of the tents and direction of the wind all combined to crowd us onto one small level area. While the rest of us muttered comments that somehow we'd have to make due, those two boys sprang into action. They slipped on their leather gloves and within five minutes had picked up the fire and moved it to a new, properly situated location. Now, with everyone fully satisfied with the design of our camp, we settled in to enjoy the evening.

Supper was enjoyed by all and after the knives, forks and one cook pot had been scrubbed, more wood was piled on the fire and we circled the chairs and coolers. This gravel bar had an abundance of driftwood and so within a short time we had a large fire burning and we, from time to time, found ourselves widening our circle as we pulled back from the heat. A large bed of shimmering coals formed below the now nearly roaring flames. As Bob threw yet another stick on the fire he announced, "It's too bad we don't have a chimney log. With all these coals, this would be a great fire for a chimney log."

"Chimney log?" I naively asked.

"Yeah, you find a hollow log, set it upright on the fire and you let the fire roar up through it."

Gene said, "I saw a hollow log on the other side of the gravel bar when we were gathering firewood, it was too big for me so I left it there."

In an instant, Bob and Gene had their flashlights out and had disappeared into the darkness. Shortly we hear a call from across the gravel bar. "We need some help here." At that point Paul, who seemed to have been restraining himself from the start of this playing-with-fire-conversation, leaped up and disappeared into the darkness. We could hear some unfamiliar "womping" sound, then some loud grunting and then a sharp exclamation, "Drop it—drop it!" This was followed by a "Damn that's heavy!" Then another call from the darkness, "Hey, we need some help here." Mike and then Russ disappeared into the darkness.

Now, I should stop here and mention that the order that the guys left the campfire pretty well represents their willingness to make mischief. I, the only one who still remained, have always been the one to suggest we stop and give this situation some thought. As a kid, running around with Bob, I was always making comments like, "Bob, do you really think you should ride your bike off the barn roof?" "Bob, are you sure you want to smoke that half used cigar you found?" "Bob, I'm afraid your dad's old pickup might throw a rod if you push it over seventy-five." Gene, in the short number of years I had known him, seemed to have the same sense of fun as Bob. Paul and Mike exhibit varying levels of troublemaking abilities based on the subject at hand. Russ is very level headed but that has never kept him from participating. I, on the other hand, have always been the stay at the fire type guy. I think I'm a fun person but I believe my main role is to make sure no one kills himself.

So anyway, after considerable grunting, the five of them emerged from the darkness bearing this fallen giant. Following a series of grunted, terse instructions from Bob, the butt end of the log was dropped into the fire and it was tipped vertical. This was followed by some rapid prancing as a couple of the guys realized that while trying to hold the log up there was some risk due to melting shoes or flaming pants. Bob and Mike, the only ones of the group who had ever seen a chimney log in action, quickly provided forked sticks as angled props to hold it upright. After it was stable, the five of them all stepped back with an air of satisfaction. The log was about six feet tall and about two feet in diameter at the bottom. A somewhat jagged bottom provided a space that Bob stoked with coals and sticks.

"What now?" I asked.

"Just wait." Bob said.

Gene reached into his cooler and pulled out a bottle of something called Cactus Juice and before the bottle had made two rounds the show had begun. Flames began to move up through the tall log and jump out the top. More stoking from below caused a shower of sparks, rather like a primitive Roman candle, to spray from the top. It had been an unusually dry summer and fall and I began to watch a few long-lived embers drift across the gravel bar into the woods just beyond. I offered a feeble suggestion that maybe the chimney log was getting a little too wild but that was ignored by everyone else. Luckily, the constant stoking necessary to produce the most dramatic fireworks required more energy than anyone was willing to provide so eventually the show settled down to a nice display of flames jumping out of and around the vertical log. After a period of time the Cactus Juice bottle was empty and its long neck was inserted in a burned out knothole in the side of the log. By carefully removing it with two sticks it could be checked from time to time as we gleefully watched the glowing red bottle neck first bend and then slowly elongate from the heat in the fiery furnace. Occasionally the log would begin to tilt in a precipitous manner but quick adjustment of the angled bracing sticks insured it stayed vertical. We enjoyed spending the next hour or so watching the flames slowly consume the vertical log. No one noticed that Bob had been absent from the circle for a while but he suddenly appeared and threw something into the white hot, glittering maw of the nearly burned out log. At the same time he emitted a stifled giggle and moved away. Mike, who clearly recognized the meaning of such a mischievous laugh asked, "What did you throw in there?" "Just an empty aerosol can of mosquito repellent", he calmly answered. At the mention of an aerosol can everyone turned on their heels and headed for the woods. We all stood in the darkness about 20 feet away from the fire for at least a minute. After another minute of the plastic topped can being in that oven, someone said, "It must be a dud." Just as we began to return to the fire a muffled explosion was heard and the chimney log teetered and then slowly fell over. It was a dramatic conclusion to a fine evening's entertainment.

The next day began in our typical leisurely way. We were on the river by mid-morning. The weather was pleasant and the fishing was good. By early afternoon Bob began to quiz the other boat owners looking for an extra battery for his trolling motor. It seems that he had scrounged up a couple of old car batteries from the shed behind his house, but these, as one might expect, had failed to hold a charge and proved to be of little use. The one good battery that he had been using for the last two days he had removed from the truck he had driven to the river. Now this battery was beginning to be a bit weak and since none of us had any good batteries to spare, he and Paul began to lag behind us.

At about 3 PM we rounded a bend and could see the low outline of some structure crossing the river ahead. This was the lock and dam we had been warned about. We pulled our boats to the right side, well away from the surging spillway on the opposite side. The dam itself was a low concrete structure covered with a large amount of tangled driftwood. At first we discussed unloading the boats and carrying them around the end of the dam on the river bank but due to the rough ground there, this did not seem practical. We decided that if we removed a few of the heaviest items from each boat we could drag the entire boat over the driftwood piled on the dam. With considerable grunting and groaning we began. This went fairly well except that dragging the boats across the dam caused the driftwood to become increasingly slippery. A little water on the thin coat of mossy scum soon caused us to slip and slide about. I have mentioned before that all of us were raised on a farm. Growing up, every time I was around a group of farm men, when they started working together as a team, they kicked the project into high gear. Then it becomes get out of the way or get run over. By the third boat we were in full farmer mode when during a combined push the boat surged forward five feet instead of the more regular three. Paul who was shoving on the stern of the boat lost his footing. His face made contact with the rear of the boat and his sunglasses broke making a cut to his face. The cut began to gush blood. As he held his handkerchief to the wound, the rest of us completed the portage of the boats. Not knowing the severity of his wound, we feared we might have to hurry him down the river for medical attention. After breaking out the first aid kit and cleaning the area we were pleased to see that it was actually quite a small cut. Like many face cuts it had produced a surprising quantity of blood but now had stopped. After applying an adhesive bandage and digging spare sunglasses out of my gear, we were on our way again.

Due to all the excitement at the lock and dam, I guess we forgot about Bob's problem with having almost no battery power left. We strung ourselves out along the river and the two boats in front failed to notice Bob and Paul falling ever farther behind. After about an hour, we saw the boat ramp ahead where Russ and I had originally planned to end our journey when we began this annual adventure five years before. We were not planning to pull off the river here this year but it seemed a good place to stop and let the others catch up. Shortly, Mike and Gene arrived but we waited and waited and no Bob and Paul. Eventually they rounded a bend and like true voyageurs of old they were paddling. They arrived and with panting voices jokingly complained of being abandoned by their buddies. Since this boat ramp was directly under a major highway with a well known service station just a few miles up the road, Bob was confident he could get his one good battery charged up. He walked up the boat ramp and found an old guy leaning against the side of his car watching the river flow past. Bob walked up to him and said. "I've had some trouble and I wonder if you could help me out." The man replied, "I'll help you anyway I can."

I'd like to take a moment and stress what a generous statement that stranger made. He didn't say, "What do you want?" or "Sorry, I've got my own problems." He said, "I'll help you anyway I can." It turned out that he was a retired gentleman who lived a number of miles away and was on his way to see a doctor at a local medical center. He knew that he was going to arrive early for his appointment and had stopped at the river access to while away some time. Bob gave him a quick run down of our story: six of us on a yearly river trip, dead battery, service station a couple of miles away, etc. and the guy said, "Grab your battery and hop in, I'll run you up to the service station."

Bob walked back to the five of us waiting at the bottom of the boat ramp and said he had found someone to help him. As he pulled the battery from the back of his boat, it was decided that with the daylight beginning to run short, Russ and I would push on and look for a campsite and

the remaining three would wait for Bob's return.
He disappeared up the ramp and we shoved off.

We had noticed all day that as we
approached the Missouri River the nature of our
river had changed. We were probably still ten
miles from the mouth but the Osage had become
wide and still, with no real gravel bars, just mud
banks. Our efforts to find a suitable camping spot
were also hampered by recreational development
along the river. Houses, cabins and docks were
frequent on both sides. As we moved farther
from the main highway these became more
scattered and eventually we found, on the west
side, a small, sloping gravel bank. Over the years,
we had become spoiled by spreading our campsites
out for thirty yards along spacious gravel bars and
gathering up piles of driftwood big enough to heat
a cabin for half a winter. Here there was barely
enough space for the tents and the fire but at least
we weren't camping in someone's yard and there
was a small amount of wood for the fire. We
gathered up the wood, removed our camping gear
and food from the boat, set up the tent in the best
area, being careful to leave room for the second
tent nearby, started the fire and sat back with a
beer to wait for the other boats to arrive.

In less than an hour they pulled up.
Recharging the battery had gone as planned. A
five minute drive to the service station, thirty
minutes with the battery on a rapid charger and a
quick drive back to the river. The old man came

down the boat ramp to chat with Paul as Bob loaded the now revived battery. (Mike and Gene were out in the river fishing.) Bob tried to offer him some money but he refused. Paul, not knowing anything about the upcoming doctor's appointment, rummaged about in his gear and pulled out a bottle of whiskey to offer the old timer a swig. Waving his hand he said, "No, no, best not have any of that—not that I have anything against it." After a couple of sincere thanks and handshakes he turned and walked up the ramp.

It was now dark so they wasted little time getting settled into camp. Gene decided this looked like a good catfish area and rigged up two poles with stink bait, clipped bells on the tip of the poles and cast them out, sticking the handle of the pole in the soft river bank and holding the tip up with a forked stick. He explained as he settled down near the fire that the tinkling of the bell would announce a fish on the line. Someone near the fire asked what kind of stink bait he had used. Gene said nothing too bad, just some slightly ripe chicken livers. Mike said, "Then why do I smell hog shit?"

Mike was right, we all smelled hog shit! Bob who raised hogs pointed out that he could just hear the quiet whir of an exhaust fan. He knew immediately what it was. Somewhere off in the darkness was a confinement hog building with a thermostatically controlled exhaust fan. Late in the day the building had finally overheated enough for the fan to come on pulling night air through the building to cool it down. Bob predicted that after the building was cooled out the fan would shut down and the smell would cease. Thankfully, he was correct.

The rest of the evening progressed pleasantly and peacefully. Gene had no luck with his fishing but since we had enough fish for supper anyway it did not matter. As the night wore on one by one we slipped off to our beds.

"Wake up, the boats are gone!" Bob's voice drifted into my sleepy brain. Russ began to stir in the sleeping bag next to me, "Huh?" The voice outside the tent was more insistent. "Wake up! The boats are gone!" At that point I was slowly coming awake and I thought to myself, well, if the boats are gone, go get them, just let me go back to sleep. I woke up enough to realize that due to the tone in Bob's voice, it would probably not be wise to say that out loud. By now I was the only one still in the tent. I moved towards the door, groped around and found, just outside the tent, my muddy shoes that I had left covered with a plastic bag. I pulled them on and as I stumbled down the dark, foggy river bank, I nearly stepped into the river. In my still sleep-fuzzed mind I thought I did not remember pitching the tent so close to the water. I looked at my watch, it was 3 AM.

The six of us were now crowded on a much narrower bank. The river had come up during the night and the boats had floated off. Over the years we had gotten in the habit of not tying the boats up because typically on an open gravel bar there is really nothing to tie them to. We always figured that if there was not substantial rain in the area we had no reason to expect a rising river. We did realize that there was a power generating dam with a huge reservoir (called the Lake of the Ozarks) upstream but had never considered that they would open the flood gates this time of year. In any case, any rationalization or excuses for not tying the boats now seemed fairly stupid. A couple of the guys got out flashlights and began to peer into the darkness and fog hoping to see something...anything.

Suddenly Mike let out a shout. He spotted a smidgen of blue on the water. All lights were poured on the same spot and the faint image of Mike's boat was outlined in the thick fog. It was about 50 feet downstream and 30 feet out. Mike started to wade out but I called him back. It was not moving, so there was time to think this through. I pointed out that I was the only one of them not fully dressed. When camping, I routinely remove my day clothing and sleep in thermal socks, gym pants and sweat shirt. I said that there was no reason for anyone to get completely soaked. I would strip off all my clothes except for my wading tennis shoes and go get the boat. My only request was that they stoked up the fire so that when I returned I could warm up. As I began to strip, someone pointed out that we needed a new fire, the old one was under about a foot of water.

I'm sure my white, naked body practically glowed in the dark as I began to wade out. Yeah, the water was cold and at that time of the early morning the air temperature must have been in the low forty's. I knew that all eyes were literally on me so I toughened up. Just as I neared the boat the water got deep enough that I had to swim the last few feet. Just before I touched the boat I got tangled up in a loose fishing line. I realized that was why the boat had not drifted away; it was caught in the line Gene had cast out for catfish the evening before. The river god had not abandoned us. Our good fortune had been caught on a nearly invisible thread. I quickly towed the boat to shore and then entered the tent to dry off and put on my clothes. When I emerged, the boys were carrying some burning branches over to the fire. Remembering what had happened the first night on the river, I asked somewhat incredulously "Are you guys moving the fire?" "No," Russ answered, "we were so anxious to get a fire going we started jumping around here and before we knew it we had two different fires going!" I was not overly chilled but I was happy for the warmth. As I stood near the fire, I listened to the plan they had developed while I was drying off and getting dressed.

The good news was in two parts, first we had one boat that we could use to find the other boats and the second was that it was Mike's with his gas outboard motor. It was old but it did run and it was the only boat with power to go rapidly downstream or upstream if that became necessary. We decided that the three boat owners, Mike, Bob and I would get in the boat and slowly move downstream looking for the wayward boats. As we stepped into Mike's boat I was confident that we would find the boats soon. We were camped on the outside of a gentle bend of the river and we knew that there were several boat docks along this side. I believed the loose boats would be caught by these protruding docks. As soon as we got on the river we realized that the fog was even thicker on the water. Anything more than 20 feet away was totally obscured. After we moved about a half of a mile downstream and past at least five different docks my heart began to sink. If the boats weren't nearby then they could be anywhere, easily hidden in the fog. Just as I was about to express this gloomy thought, the beam from Bob's flashlight played across the shiny bow of my boat. It was slowly bumping its way downstream but had kept close to shore. By mutual agreement I got in her, turned her around and slowly began to move towards our campsite. Within five seconds,

Bob and Mike disappeared into the fog as they continued the search.

It took me a surprisingly long time to make my way back upstream. The nearly stagnant current of the day before had been replaced with the increased water flow of the rising river. It took me about 45 minutes to return to the campsite and by that time the early glow of morning illuminated the valley. I was pleased to see some relief expressed in the faces of my shore-bound comrades as I first appeared through the now lifting fog. I explained the circumstances of finding my boat and expressed the hope that in the daylight and lessening fog Bob's boat would soon be found.

The boys had not been idle while I was gone. The coffee pot was under full steam and I appreciatively filled my cup. I made some general comments about the confined nature of our campground and they pointed to a stick they had placed at the water's edge just an hour ago. It was now submerged under six inches of water. They had spent the last hour retrieving whatever sunken camping and fishing gear they could locate. I was particularly pleased that my cooking grill had been recovered. It was clear that a number of items had floated off or sunk but until we were back together a complete inventory would not be possible.

Since there was little else to do except wait, we decided that breakfast might as well be started. Just as the sausage was finished we heard the whine of an outboard motor downriver. Anxious eyes peered into the last wisps of fog hoping to see Mike appear. It was him. Moving upstream at full throttle the bow of his empty boat was rising precariously out of the water. Bob was not with him so we hoped he had good news. I guess our anxious pose on the river bank caused Mike to call out as soon has he throttled back his motor, "We found Bob's boat." After landing and with a full plate of sausage, eggs and toast pushed into his hands he told us his story.

They had continued downstream for at least another two miles scanning and searching the dark river. They found one of their floating buckets of gear and one of Mike's insulated boots that had somehow turned upside down trapping air in the bottom causing it to float. As a gentle fog-diffused light began to break over the river their attention was directed to a dark image in the center of the river. Like the ghost ship the Flying Dutchman, Bob's boat emerged from the fog moving under full sail towards the Missouri River. Mike fired up the outboard and they gave chase. They caught up with the boat literally within sight of the mighty river. If they had not spotted the boat when they did, within another thirty minutes the boat would have entered the Missouri and probably never would have been found. As they pulled alongside they nervously commented to each other how much the boat appeared to have been recently piloted by ghosts. The motor tiller was extended, both seats were in place, one fishing pole trailed a line in the river and a can of beer in its foam cooler sat nearby. That did not prevent Bob from quickly climbing aboard and soon Mike was towing him upstream. This is when the instability of Mike's empty boat began to cause the bow of his boat to buck wildly. They stopped, discussed their options and decided that Bob and his boat would just slow Mike's return to our camp so Bob would stay there with his boat and wait for us to come downstream to him. So that's how Mike ended up returning alone.

Relieved that all was going to end well we finished our breakfast, I wrapped a sausage sandwich in aluminum foil for Bob and within a short time the tents were down and the boats loaded. Soon enough, we caught up with Bob and as he munched his sandwich we were treated to his version of their experiences. Just ahead on our left was the broad water of the Missouri and on our right was the boat ramp. A brief discussion was held to determine if we dare approach the big river any more closely. All votes were that we had had enough for this year. If the White Trash River Boys were going to have any more adventures, they would have to wait until next year.

CHAPTER FIVE

A Perfect Day

Since Russ and I were the only two that floated the first leg of the river below Bagnell Dam, it was not a surprise that the group voted to begin the journey over so the later arriving members could see all the sections of the river. So a year after the boats got away from us, we had once again returned to the Osage River. This time we bypassed the boat ramp at the campground where the batteries had crashed and burst and instead chose a Department of Conservation ramp slightly closer to the outwash of the dam. As is often the case for the White Trash River Boys things don't go as planned. When Gene and I pulled up, Paul had already arrived and was sitting in his truck near the entrance to the river access. Behind him was a sign on the shoulder of the road saying, "River Access Closed." We could hear some large machine running inside the grounds and so Gene and Paul walked in to see what was up. I stayed at the entrance to wait for the rest of the crew to arrive. Shortly Bob, Mike and Russ arrived and they decided to drive back up the highway and search for another put-in location. Within a few minutes, Gene and Paul returned and said that there was an equipment operator rolling a new layer of asphalt on the parking lot. It had been quite dry all fall and Gene suggested to the operator that they could get to the boat ramp by driving across the grass without even getting on the new asphalt. The operator said, "Go for it."

Gene was hauling my boat so he quickly drove to the ramp and we soon had it unloaded and in the water. About the time we were done, we noticed Mike waving to us from a gravel bar on the other side of the river and we motioned for them to return. Within a short time Gene and Paul had parked their trucks along the shoulder of the road just outside the access and Bob, Mike and Russ pulled up to the ramp and we began unloading Bob and Mike's boats. Just then some guy drove up, stepped out of his truck and told us in a huff we could not launch our boats here and we would have to pull our equipment out of the river and leave. We mentioned that the operator running the roller said that we would not hurt anything by launching here but this made no impression on this guy who insisted in a louder voice that we needed to clear out. At this point, two of the boats were fully loaded and in the river and the third was nearly so. While Mike pleasantly talked to this guy about this being our annual trip, where we would be floating, taking out, etc., Bob quickly drove his truck up to where we had parked the others. By now the guy was emphatic that we could not launch here—the sign said "River Access Closed" and by God that meant closed—we needed to get our boats out of the river and get ourselves out of here. When I saw Bob briskly walking towards us from where he had parked his truck, I climbed in the back of my boat and motioned to Russ to shove us off. Seeing this, Bob never broke stride and stepped from the boat ramp into his boat and Paul pushed them into the river. With the guy still fussing and fuming, Mike entered his boat and continued to counter the guy's anger with pleasant comments about the river and questions about the quality of the fishing in the area. Gene loaded the last couple of items in the boat and pushed off. With the guy standing on the boat ramp with a scowl on his face and his hands on his hips, Mike called out, "Thanks for your help. Have a nice day!" and we turned our boats into the river.

The boat ramp was only a short distance from the dam so while the other two boats headed downstream Russ and I headed towards the dam. Since we had been unable to do it five years ago, we wanted to start our journey at the dam, or least as close to the dam as the warning sign suggested we approach. Dams are a popular thing for environmentalists to condemn but in my opinion any dam is impressive when viewed from below. Bagnall dam was completed in 1939 and it has a retro-chic art deco styling. I've seen photos taken when the work was underway and mules and Model A Fords are prominently included. The workmen of that age are also present in the old photographs—posing in their floppy-caps and bib-overalls. When they stand straight and tall in front of their handiwork their faces show their confidence in hard work. And now over 70 years later most of those men are dead but a monument to their hard work lives on.

The turbulent water below the dam is noted as a good fishing spot and Russ and I did pull out a couple of small ones but hooked no keepers. Our companions had disappeared around a bend almost an hour earlier so we thought it best to follow along.

We proceeded fairly slowly. It was warm and a bit breezy for October but we enjoyed making a serious effort to fish as we floated. It was probably another hour before we caught sight of the other two boats in the distance. Both boats were pulled onto the shore at the end of a straight stretch about a quarter mile ahead. As we approached we could see standing figures moving about something white lying on the gravel. It looked as if someone had collapsed and the others were attempting first aid. As we drew nearer, we were relieved to see the invalid was Mike's outboard motor.

The first couple of years that Mike joined us he had an antique outboard motor. It was so old you had to wrap the starter rope around a pulley at the top of the motor. This was a charming, old fashioned activity to watch from a distance but the person in the front of the boat had to lean forward in his seat to prevent being whipped like a mutinous sailor by the flying, knotted rope. Two years ago the motor sort of caught on fire. Not bad—nothing a little splashing with river water could not extinguish. Last year, he arrived with this white, five horse power motor. He bought it at a garage sale for 20 bucks, took it home and after a little cleaning it started right up. The previous motor had been about 50 years old and this one was only about 30 years old. It was considered a significant upgrade for the White Trash River Boys.

The first thing they asked me as we stepped onto the shore was what tools I had with me. As I handed over a metal ammo box that held a bunch of junk, a spark plug wrench, rusty pliers and two broken down screwdrivers, Mike and Gene, the main surgeons, returned to their patient. Bob, who was acting as operating room nurse, informed us that the prop had hit some unknown submerged obstruction and now would function only in reverse. Normally, our main method of propulsion is our battery trolling motors and we only rely on Mike's outboard when we need to move upstream or make faster progress downstream. Mike had been running it this afternoon because from time to time, an ever increasing headwind was making it difficult to make forward progress with his tiny trolling motor.

At this time we had probably progressed four miles down from the put-in and based on our previous experiences on this river we assumed we were pretty well in the middle of nowhere. All of a sudden something fell from the sky and landed nearly in the middle of us. Our reaction was what you might have expected if someone had yelled "Incoming!" We all threw our hands up over our heads and scattered apart. My first thought was to cuss Paul for lobbing a rock into our midst when Russ reached down and held up a golf ball. This caused us all to begin to discuss rather stupidly where a golf ball could have come from when high above us on the top of the river bank a voice called out to us, "Have you seen a golf ball?" We threw the ball back up to the guy who seemed as surprised to see six wild looking guys down by the river as we were surprised to see a chubby guy in a sweater holding a golf club. Seeing the outboard motor laying on its side he kindly asked if we needed any help. We held a quick discussion to determine how much trouble a sick outboard might cause us and decided to decline. We were, after all, heading downstream and we thought we could make it outboard motor or no.

The operating personnel continued their efforts, Russ and I relaxed and Paul began to climb about the river bank looking for golf balls. After about twenty minutes he came down and emptied all the pockets in his army coat into a bucket. He counted out 26 golf balls! The surgeons announced that they could not repair the patient stating not a lack of expertise but inadequate tools (a common manly excuse). Mike again expressed doubts about being able to keep up with the other two boats considering the ever increasing headwind. Someone asked could he motor down the river stern first if necessary? He said that he had already tried that and too much water poured over the transom. Someone asked could we mount the motor on the bow of the boat and pull the boat downstream? Now that was the sort of suggestion that caused each member of our group to spring into action. All of us enjoy a mechanical challenge. Once we began the task, critical scraps of wood, essential bolts and necessary pieces of wire appeared like the fishes and loaves at that famous picnic on the mountain. Soon enough we had the outboard secured to the bow and with Mike now in the front and Gene in the back they pushed off. With one hand confidently on the tiller Mike began pulling the starter rope with the other. After some unsuccessful pulls followed by some fine tuning of the choke, the motor started, creating a blue cloud which they left behind as they smoothly motored downstream. With great satisfaction we returned to our boats and followed behind.

Mike and Gene motored out of sight around the next bend while we stayed back and continuing to fish as we slowly moved downriver. After a couple of hours we saw them ahead on a gravel bar pulling firewood together indicating that they had found a camping spot for the night. By this time it was nearly sunset. The afternoon had progressed evermore cloudy and windy. By the time the tents were up and the fire going, we heard a rumble of thunder from a long, horizontal, blue-black cloud visible in the southwest. While a few of us expressed a hope that the cloud would pass harmlessly over us, Gene who spends more time outdoors than the rest of us assured us that in less than half an hour it was going to be raining hard. The fire had not progressed to the proper stage to cook supper, but I decided to get the steaks cooked as quickly as I could anyway. While everyone else rummaged around for their rain gear, I positioned the grill over the hottest part of the fire and threw on the steaks. Just as the first drops arrived Russ came over with my poncho and a plastic tarp. I always bring that tarp to cover the gear in the boat if it is raining while we are on the river. Soon the drops increased to what my dad would have described as a real nice shower and from that moved into a toad strangler. The boys were holding the plastic tarp above the fire as we tried to cajole our steaks from rare to medium rare. By now each man had a plate, fork and knife in hand and one by one each chose a steak, grabbed a handful of corn chips from the bag and disappeared into one of the tents. Soon only Bob and I were left in the deluge. I was satisfied with my steak but Bob, who is willing to gut and skin any animal that you would throw down in front of him, is squeamish about any blood on his dinner plate. I removed my steak and covered it with a plastic bag while Bob continued to flip his steak. The problem was with only two of us holding the tarp above the fire we continually struggled to prevent the streams of water flowing off the tarp from dumping into the fire. As the power of the flames began to wane under the rain's onslaught, he finally gave up on the grill, threw it to one side and laid the steak directly on the remaining embers. After a few more minutes he announced that it was done, grabbed the steak bare-handed from the fire (if it could even be called a fire at this point) and brushing off the stuck bits of embers with the backside of his fork threw the steak on his plate and we retreated into the tents. We had put up three tents that evening so I entered a tent occupied by Gene. In our haste to prepare supper neither of us removed a flashlight from our gear so I felt my way around the darkness, sat down on the edge of someone's cot and since it was pitch black, we ate our steaks and chips like blind men, without benefit of fork and knife, touching our way over our plate searching for that one last chip or the misplaced bone that we were certain had one last morsel to gnaw.

The thunder and lightening crashed for about a half hour and then the downpour abated to a hard drizzle. We could hear a few hardy souls moving about the camp opening coolers to grab a beer and once again dragging firewood onto the fire. We double checked our rain gear and went outside to join the others. We had a pleasant evening visiting with each other while we struggled to keep the fire going but by ten the fire was on its own and we were all in our sleeping bags.

It rained and drizzled through the night and next morning. It paused just enough so we could enjoy breakfast. With the proper rain gear, floating and fishing are not bad as long as it is a drizzle or less and fortunately as the day progressed the rain moved on through and by mid-afternoon we had permanently removed our rain gear. Then we began to pile on clothing as the wind shifted to the north and the temperature continued to drop. In spite of the cold, we had better than average luck with fishing, with Bob pulling out an especially nice large mouth bass. The change in weather seemed to also bring out the bald eagles. At one point we spotted four riding high on the cold wind. There is a Sioux saying that whenever you see an eagle your thoughts should soar to higher levels.

Almost every year at some point along the river, Russ and I stop to hunt arrowheads in some farmer's plowed field. We can usually find some flakes or broken pieces but we've never come up with anything whole. A couple of years back, Bob found a nice arrowhead just as he stepped from his boat onto a gravel bar. This year it was too muddy to walk any fields but late afternoon we saw a long cut bank ahead on the right hand side. It was unusual in that the normally level field had a gentle bump or rise that had been partially cut away by the river. I told Russ that if I had been an Indian camping centuries ago along this river, I would have chosen just that little bump for my camp. We stopped, tied up the boat and began walking the steep cut bank back and forth. Some flakes and chips were found indicating that my instincts were good but we turned up no arrowheads. After both of us walked over the area, I told Russ that I was enjoying stretching my legs and asked him to return to the boat while I walked along the bank. I caught up with him about an eighth of a mile downstream. When I approached him I pulled from my pocket four nice little arrowheads I had found along the cut-bank just another fifty yards downstream from where we had given up our search.

Since Russ was in the back of the boat, I took the front seat and we proceeded downstream. We had trailed well behind the others almost all day and now that the sun was going down we felt we should hurry to catch up. Within a short while we rounded a bend and some distance straight ahead we saw that our comrades had already chosen our campsite. It was situated in front of a high, long, blacked-streaked, gray cliff. One tent was already up. The center of the scene was the newly started campfire. It was creating, as any new fire will, a large amount of smoke. As blue-brown smoke drifted heavily across the river, two of our companions were visible making contributions to the large driftwood/firewood stack. Behind us, the clearing sky was streaked orange and blue, causing the entire scene to be washed in a streaming golden light.

For me, sitting in the front of my boat with those four arrowheads in my pocket, I suddenly felt a special mystery overtake the campsite. Time leaped backwards. The aluminum boats on the shore became dugout canoes, the beer coolers became bundles of pelts and the camouflage jackets became buffalo skin robes. No other part of the scene had to change, for I am confident that the appearance of the slender willows and strong sycamores at the base of the steep bluffs were timeless. I kept my vision to myself. After we had stepped ashore and as I showed the others what I had found, I noticed that as I held the four arrowheads in my palm, I had instinctively pointed them to the four cardinal directions. I again felt the river of time flow back upon itself. With daylight fading fast, a camp to be made and a supper to be prepared, thoughts of such strong medicine would have to wait.

A few years back, a tradition developed that one of us would read aloud after we ate supper on the second night. It started when Russ read to us a short story by Willa Cather entitled "The Enchanted Bluff". The next year I read a chapter from Longfellow's *Hiawatha*. (Some of our White Trash River Boys favorite readings can be found in the appendix of this book.) The reading for this year was a selection from John Neihardt's *Black Elk Speaks*. It has several pages that I call "Black Elk's Prayer".

After the reading, the conversation returned to the arrowheads. Bob identified one of the points as a style known as an Afton point, used by a people who lived about 2500 years ago. The subject of the culture of ancient Native Americans is a topic that this group loves to return to time and time again. I particularly enjoy expressing opinions that I have formed after reading some book or observing some artifact. These opinions are always challenged based upon some differing experience of the group. That evening's conversation soon changed from the more mundane topics, such as how these great people lived and hunted, to the spiritual. From the beliefs of these ancients we began to discuss personal philosophies. Some in our group are traditionalists who cannot seem to grasp any God who is not a bearded old man sitting on a cloud. Russ and I spent some time trying to convince them of a larger view of God, a God that pervades everything. These traditionalists just shook their heads when in a late night inspiration, Russ held up a rock and announced, "God is this rock!"

The night was clear and cold as was the next day. We faced into a stiff, north wind all day. The warm coffee in the thermos gave out at about 11 AM so we stopped, built a small fire in a sheltered area on a gravel bar and brewed some more. While we were savoring our coffee in the sunshine, we discovered a small hollow stick. It was placed upright on the fire and held with some small forked sticks. Soon we were enjoying a miniature chimney log.

When we returned to the water, my boat led our companions downstream. A too-deep-blue sky arched over us and as we looked back, bright sunlight flashed off sloping water and waving fishing rods. Ahead a mother deer and her two spotted babies refreshed themselves in the water. Eventually their white tails flashed their surprise at seeing men on their river. Again, I could sense a special mystery. The luminous sun behind us pervaded the earth with a crisp, quiet energy. Everything seemed connected.

The day was filled with little fish and large enjoyment. By mid-afternoon we had stepped from our boats the last time. Most of our group left to retrieve the trucks at the put-in. Mike and I waited quietly for their return. I found a sunny spot and lay down on the grass. I recalled Russ' comment from last night. In my mind I completed his statement. God is this rock, this grass, these trees, this sky, these comrades. God is this river!

Reclining on the grass, finally out of the wind, with the sun pouring on me, waiting for the return of my river brothers, which will signal the end of this annual trek, I realized that this had been...a...perfect...day.

CHAPTER SIX

Campfire Stories

I've mentioned that we have some pretty serious conversations around the campfire but I don't want to mislead you. We don't spend all evening discussing St. Augustine's understanding of God or reviewing the political and historical implications of our involvement in the Middle East. The vast majority of the time we talk about "guy stuff" which is of course hunting, fishing, sports, traveling and often talk about really nothing at all.

At least once every year we try to get someone to tell a story. They relate an experience that they think we might enjoy hearing or repeat a story they heard around some other campfire. If it is a good story, every few years we'll ask to hear it again. Over time the story becomes polished and is considered a classic.

The secret to a classic campfire story is that the teller must make it his personal story. It should be told in the first person and minor details should be altered to fit the storyteller's life. If it is a scary story, it is best if the location of the story's events occur in the immediate vicinity. A couple of the White Trash Boys who are fathers of teenagers have told the "Momo" story at hayrides and other outside events to prevent boys and girls from slipping off away from the fire for make-out sessions.

Here I've included four of my favorite campfire stories. They are not all my own stories but following my own advice, I've changed them to fit my personal experiences.

"Momo"

The telling of this story is improved if you have an accomplice to provide some of his own "facts" in support of your tale.

"A campfire is a cozy and safe place but if you take a few steps into the darkness you begin to feel uneasy. In Missouri, for generations we have repressed these instinctive fears because our intellect told us the scariest animal we were likely to encounter away from the security of our fire was a feisty raccoon or a rabid skunk. Things have begun to change. Reports of bear and cougar are becoming more common and it is likely that in the next few years someone we personally know will have an encounter with one of those potentially dangerous animals. But what about the scariest denizen of the night, a creature that has been glimpsed in the darkest corners of the wild for years and years? Is it an animal, is it a human or is it some distant cousin? In this part of the country he is known as Momo. It's a cute name but you should know its short for Missouri Monster. There's no doubt he's directly related to the Northwest coast's Sasquatch, the Texas Bigfoot and Florida's Skunk Ape. Where there are deep, wild places this monster lurks."

"Momo is described as a tall, hairy, bipedal beast. He's six to seven feet tall, has long brown or reddish brown hair over his entire body. His hair is usually described as muddy or matted. His round head sits atop his body with no noticeable neck. His long arms reach nearly to his knees. When describing Momo, one important item must not be omitted, his smell. Bad is the most commonly used adjective but more descriptive terms might be rotten, moldy leaves or stagnant water."

"My house sits up on a ridge that marks the change from open prairie to the rolling hills and river valleys that stretch unbroken south and west into the Arkansas Ozarks and from there into the wilds of eastern Oklahoma and Texas. In those hills and hollers there are thousands and thousands of acres where humans rarely set foot. It's well known that many animals utilize the boundaries between prairie and forest because these areas are rich in plant and animal life. That's why I believe near where I live some creature, some large creature, wanders the forest. Is it

Momo or something else? Let me tell you these facts and I'll let you decide for yourself."

"Fact #1—A short time after I moved onto my land, I was visiting with one of my new neighbors. He was an old man whose family had lived on the adjoining 80 acres since it was first platted back in 1832. We were talking about an old abandoned quarry that was located on the back of his property when he admitted that he rarely went down there at night and never went there during the dark of the moon. This surprised me, this old man being an experienced farmer and an active deer and turkey hunter. When I asked him to explain, all he said was, 'Down there is something that is just not right.'

"Fact #2—The first years after I moved into my house, I had this dog. Her name was Senna. She was a good dog and a smart dog. She liked to run. Often on weekends she and I would take off wandering over the countryside. If I walked five miles, she probably ran fifty. She would run deer, turkey, rabbits, squirrels and sometimes run just for the sheer joy of it. As we walked, she made long circling loops so that about every 10 minutes she would swing past me to sort of check in and then off she would go again. I can tell you that anytime we got within 200 yards of that old man's quarry she would come and stay right beside me, her ears straight up with the hair on the back of her neck standing."

"Fact #3—One late winter afternoon, I was helping my neighbor round up her goats, which had crossed her fence onto my land. The back of her land is near the old quarry I mentioned earlier. She began to talk about some huge foot prints she had seen in the snow a few weeks earlier. She thought it was very strange. She understood that as snow melts any track in the snow will grow in size but the tracks she had seen were in crisp fresh snow and the outline of toes was clearly visible. Someone or something had been walking around in the snow with bare feet."

"Fact #4—A few weeks later while I was out hunting mushrooms, I found the carcass of a stray dog. Most of the meaty part had been eaten. It appeared that the chest cavity had been opened and the heart and liver removed. The head and neck were intact but what was particularly unsettling was the head was twisted around backwards and was nearly touching the top of the shoulders. It was as if some beast had snapped its neck."

"I don't know if all this proves that I have Momo for a neighbor. I've told these stories to others and they have suggested a black bear or cougar. I don't think a bear could or would snap the neck of a dog and if there was a cougar in the area, I don't think my neighbor's goats would be safe. Whatever is living down there is too smart to eat someone's livestock. The last story I'll tell is that I've seen it or at least seen something I cannot explain."

"Fact #5—The Saturday before last Easter I was walking about a half mile south of my house and I saw a large creature moving quickly through the woods about 100 yards in front of me. It looked to be about six feet tall with a reddish coat. It was not running on four feet but on two. That was all I saw but that was enough! I turned around and went home and spent the rest of the day inside the house watching TV."

"Happy Thanksgiving"

"It was a beautiful early November day and I was enjoying a bright, clear morning in the woods. There had been a light frost last night. As I walked briskly up a south facing hill, the early morning sun was pouring its energy into the landscape. As the frost was melting and the dew was drying, smoke-like wisps of fog rose from any damp surface which was being sufficiently warmed. As I neared the top, I heard two cluck-clucks of a hen turkey and I instinctively slowed my pace so as not to spook her. I cautiously eased around one large tree and scanned a slightly open area just ahead for the hen. No sign of her so I slowly moved forward. Suddenly, something was very wrong. I was hit in the chest with such force I was knocked off my feet. I tried to stand but all I could do was flail around on the ground. That's when I noticed there was something sticking in my side. It was a long straight shaft. I was shot! Someone shot me with an arrow! I tried to call for help but I didn't have the strength to make a sound. I was suddenly so tired. I needed to close my eyes. The last thing I saw was a man. He looked like a walking bush. I was so tired…so tired. I could hear his feet rustling the leaves as he walked towards me."

"Then I was in the in-between-time. Everything there was very faint. I don't know what was real and what was not. I thought I heard voices. I seemed to be flying but I know I wasn't moving. And then there was the cold—a deep, dark cold. I was frozen to the bone."

"I realize now that I died that morning. In my beautiful woods I died. Sure, I would have liked to live longer but if it was my time to go, I can't complain. I was in good health and enjoyed my life. I mean, I could have fallen over dead from a heart attack in those woods and never been found. I would have ended up as worm food. As it is, I'm content. I'd even say happy. I had the joy of living free and wild and in the end, I was invited as the guest of honor at Thanksgiving dinner."

"The Man with the Silver Hand"
This story requires an accomplice to quietly excuse himself from the fire circle about halfway through the story.

"Everyone from Missouri knows that Mark Twain grew up in Missouri as Samuel Clemens and as a young man was a Mississippi River pilot. You might not know that when the Civil War began and river traffic was halted he joined a local militia for a short while and then after deciding that soldiering was not for him headed west to the gold fields of Nevada and then on to California. You might be familiar with his story 'The Man with the Golden Arm', which he enjoyed telling many years later. He placed his story in California but I can tell you with certainty that the story actually took place in Missouri and was originally known as the 'Man with the Silver Hand'. I know this because my family has been telling the true version of the story for over 150 years. We even know that Mr. Clemens first heard the story in a saloon in Jefferson City from the brother of my great-great grandpa."

"The true story goes like this. Fortuna, Missouri is now just a little town but many years ago it was much larger due to a successful lead mine. There was one local man, named Ben Brown who believed that he could make his fortune in Fortuna by mining not lead but silver. He believed this because when he arrived in the area during a January snow storm he was saved from freezing to death by an old man who shared his crude cabin with him. This crippled old man was a Cherokee Indian and after Ben got a job at the lead mine, he would occasionally take coffee, sugar or other supplies to him as a thank you. During one visit in late spring he found the old man dead in his bed. Ben buried the old guy. Before he left he didn't hesitate to pick through the man's meager belongings. There was one cook pot, one coffee pot and one blanket worth keeping. It was only later when he returned to his room in Fortuna did he discover a small bundle inside the coffee pot. When unwrapped, he found several light gray stones each having a thick, wavy, shiny layer of silver."

"So that's how Ben began to search for the silver mine. The old man said when his people were forced westward on what became known as the Trail of Tears, he slipped away, traveled north and settled in this small valley. After that he stayed put. Ben was convinced that the mine had to be nearby. Eventually he did find the source of the silver and by mining some of it on the sly and selling the ore in St. Louis, he was able was able to return and buy the land and work the mine openly. The main vein of ore in the mine was lead and he was able to keep his real wealth hidden because he always sold his silver in St. Louis. He told the buyer that the ore was coming from the far west."

"He named the mine 'The Cherokee Mine' and became quite rich even though the mine was small. To protect his secret, he kept it a one man operation. As with most men, once he had land and money he began to think he needed a wife. The ore buyer in St. Louis had a lovely daughter. Indeed, the muscular, wealthy miner was attractive to the young lady and after a period of courtship they were married. Ben was happy with his new wife and was confident that he had chosen well. Since she had come from a wealthy family he did not fear she had married him for his money. On the day of their marriage they boarded a paddle wheeler for a month's stay in New Orleans. Upon their return, the honeymoon abruptly ended when, outside of Fortuna, she laid eyes on the tiny cabin in the valley which was to become her home. As you can imagine, how do you keep her down at the mine after she's seen gay New Orleans?"

"She began to hate her new life and as she saw him day after day in his dirty work clothes, she began to despise him. Her distaste for him only deepened after an accident at the mine—a jack slipped and Ben's right hand was crushed. The hand had to be removed and after it healed, Ben had a silversmith make a hand of silver. It was really some hand or quite handsome—if you will excuse the pun. It had carved fingernails and ridges to represent veins. It even had small lines engraved on it to represent the hairs that once were on his hand. As you might imagine the lovely young wife shuddered every time Ben approached the marital bed. This uneasy life was only made worse when Ben hired a strong, good-looking young man to help work at the mine."

"Now, there was no evidence that there was foul play but quite soon Ben fell ill and shortly was on his death bed. As he looked back on his life he had no regrets. In his final days his wife was caring and kind and he once again believed she loved him. He was happy to leave all his earthly riches to her and dictated his will to a local lawyer stating as much. His only request was to be buried with his silver hand. She would have all his money and so surely she could honor his request."

"After his death, things moved quickly. Of course, the young worker moved from the work shed to his boss' bed. And with all the money they had, why work at all or even stay in Fortuna? The silver ore had played out. Why not sell the mine and move to St. Louis where they could enjoy the life they deserved?"

"A short time after they settled in St. Louis, her father became ill. In spite of careful nursing by his daughter (or because of, according to some local gossips) he passed away. An inheritance piled on top of another inheritance means money and plenty of it. It's surprising how fast you can spend plenty of money if you really make an effort. It wasn't long before they were running up debts and decided to head west. They barely had money enough to begin their journey and in Jefferson City were removed from the steamboat because they couldn't continue to pay. They sold most of their personal items and began to walk west. After a couple of days on foot they began to talk of nothing but Ben's silver hand. A few more days' journey and they were within sight of the Cherokee Mine. Ben had asked to be buried on a hill overlooking the mine entrance so it was one night of digging and then refilling the grave and they had the silver hand.

"If this was a modern tale, Ben would rise from the grave, track down his faithless wife and her lover and kill them both but that did not happen. It is true that things did not end well for the young husband. He was killed in a knife fight during a poker game in Virginia City. Her story ends on a better note. She traveled on to San Francisco and married a tailor who was getting rich making work pants for the local miners. They lived happily ever after."

"I can tell you that Ben did not rest peacefully without his silver hand. Where the Cherokee Mine was once located is now the site of the Missouri Department of Conservation's Lake Manitou. They unknowingly placed the campground over Ben's grave. Often when people camp there, in the dead of night, they hear a voice like this in the wind. *At this point in a low windy voice I begin to call out.* 'Who, who-ooo, who took my silver hand? Who-oo took my silver hand?' *While I continue to call, I stand and begin to move around the campfire. While everyone is watching me; my accomplice quietly approaches one person from behind and suddenly grabs that person by the shoulders, shakes them and shouts.* 'You took my silver hand! You have my silver hand! Give it back! Give it back!' *This will cause screams and laughter to erupt around the campfire.*

"Grandfather Eagle"

"A few years back the White Trash Boys were on our annual fishing-floating trip. We were on one of the middle sections of the Osage River. It was our second day on the river and we were beginning to become concerned about a long dark row of clouds that was moving in from the southwest. As we discussed the ominous clouds, Russ pointed to three bald eagles, two adults and one juvenile. They were soaring on the powerful winds just ahead of the storm. As they flew off, the wind began whipping white caps on the river, the rain began to drop and lightning crashed above. We were fortunate that at the same time we saw some metal steps leading from the river up to a level field above. We tied up our boats and climbed up. There we discovered a small river cabin but more importantly a roofed over picnic area. By this time, the rain was rolling past us in sheets and the lighting was flashing directly overhead. We dashed under the shelter and sat on the picnic table. Someone asked, 'Where's Bob?' 'He's probably just getting a beer.' And sure enough, a few moments later he arrived carrying a small cooler in his left hand and a small white and gray object in his right. It was a small, nicely formed arrowhead. He had spotted it on the gravel just as he stepped from the boat. We all admired it as he passed it around. The beers were distributed and we sat back waiting for the rain to abate. It rained like the dickens for about twenty minutes"

"As the rain began to let up we noticed someone walking across the field. When he noticed us he turned and worked his way down to our location. Soon he joined us under the shelter. We quickly explained who we were and why we were bunched under this shelter. He introduced himself as Mr. Wakon. He was wearing a brown canvas coat with a hood over brown bib overalls. In spite of his farmer type clothes, he had a dramatic appearance due to his long, white shoulder length hair which was combed straight back. His look was further enhanced by a long sharply beaked nose. He said he knew the owner of this little place and assured us the owner would not mind us being there. We offered him a beer, which he declined. On the picnic table was the arrowhead that Bob had found. Bob picked it up and showed it to the old man. Mr. Wakon handled it carefully and gave it back. He then reached up to wooden shelf near the rafters and pulled down an old cigar box. Inside were many chert flakes and some broken and whole arrowheads. As we studied them, he stated all these were found in the immediate area."

"For a while we made small talk about fishing the river, farming and the weather. Russ mentioned the three eagles we saw earlier. Mr. Wakon said that he often sees those three eagles. He said there is a fourth, an old male—the granddaddy of them all. He has been here years and years. I mentioned that some Native Americans believed that when you see a soaring eagle you should turn your thoughts away from the matters of this earth. A soaring eagle should remind us to turn our thoughts to our Father above. The old man said that many years ago he had heard the same thing. After a moment's silence we observed that the rain had slowed considerably. He bid us goodbye and started back the way he had come. Suddenly, he stopped and returned to us under the shelter. 'You fellows seem a little different than many who visit this river', he said. 'Let me tell you a story.' He told us about an Indian village that once stood on this site thousands of years ago. He spoke with such sincerity and intensity that none of us interrupted with questions or comments. He said that it had about twenty lodges, not teepees, but curved structures made of bent saplings and covered with woven mats of grass which at that time grew plentiful in this field just to the east. Swinging his arm to the west, he indicated the lodges were strung out more or less along a low ridge now visible in the stubble of the soybean field. Near the center of the village was a single pole and hanging from the pole were four long strips of buffalo hide each one a different color. The black one represents the west, where the Thunder Beings live. They provide the rain that sustains all life. The white represents the north, from whence comes the cold scouring wind that cleans the earth and prepares it for renewed growth. The red is the east, the source of wisdom that comes with the morning star. And finally, the yellow strip of hide represents the south, the power of summer, the power to grow. He said the pole from which those four streamers flew represented the point where the four corners of the universe come together, a special, sacred place of great energy. Due to their beliefs, he said, the village prospered there for many decades. Even when the floods came, the people simply moved up the hill and waited because they knew the river replenished their farmland and next year's crops of beans and squash would be better. With time people change, so of course, cultures change also. Eventually the farming village was abandoned for a more mobile hunting lifestyle. Since then, the site has only been occupied by those who are here to enjoy the hunting or fishing. Mr. Wakon said he often comes to this area of the river and circles the site of the old village. He said he still feels the power of this place—this place where the four corners of the universe come together.

"By the time he quit speaking, the rain had mostly stopped. He left us with this farewell, 'May there be only good between you.' As we also prepared to leave, Bob picked up the cigar box, placed the arrowhead he had found on the gravel bar inside the box, gently closed the lid and returned it to the shelf. We returned to our boats and proceeded downriver. Within an hour the powerful mid-afternoon sun was out, shining bright and clear. Suddenly, a shadow passed over our boat. Russ and I looked up and directly ahead of us circled a large eagle, its white head and tail shining in the sun. It moved quickly lower and then flying directly upstream passed over all three of our boats. At some distance behind us, it curved gracefully and landed on dead branch in a huge sycamore tree. It shook both wings twice and then sat motionlessly, proudly. Russ said, 'That's not one of the eagles we saw earlier.' I said, 'You're right, that's a very different eagle— that's the granddaddy of them all.'

CHAPTER SEVEN

A Sinking Feeling

I have to say I'm certain that none of us wanted anything but another pleasant float. It was true that in the last several years of our annual outing we hadn't been coming home with any exciting stories. It had been a number of years since the boats had floated off. Every fall since then the weather has been beautiful; the flowing water appealing, the fishing good and the camaraderie even better but a routine had set in. When we returned home our wives and families having already heard about conked-out motors, chimney logs and blackened catfish fillets, politely asked how the trip went, wanted to know the latest updates about everyone's family and then that was pretty much it. After having floated the Osage River several more times, we made a change to the Gasconade River. The Gasconade is a clearer, smaller, faster river but is still located in central Missouri. Its headwaters are in the Ozarks and it enters the Missouri River just east of the center part of the state. This year we were in our fourth year of being on this river. None of us gave it much thought when as we visited around the campfire the first night, Russ said that while he was kissing his wife goodbye she made some comment about his failure to come home with any good stories. I mentioned that Janet had made a similar comment.

Actually, Bob and Mike had already provided, before the float had even begun, a story to tell our wives. As usual, we planned to meet at the boat launch at 3 PM. As we had for the last several years, Paul and I were riding with Gene. This had become our routine because a few years back he had bought a new boat. He had been talking about buying a boat for a number of years and it seemed one crossed his path that he found irresistible. It was a new 16' jon boat that was 55" wide at the beam. It was a leviathan compared to our boats. The boat and trailer were new and on the back was a nice used 8 horse Evinrude outboard motor. We found it convenient to transport my boat by setting it inside his boat. This year we had stopped to pick up Russ who was, as usual, leaving his car at the take-out ramp. We arrived at the put-in ramp about twenty minutes behind schedule and were surprised to find Bob and Mike weren't there. Gene backed down the ramp and we got the boats in the water and everything loaded. About 45 minutes late Bob and Mike pulled up in their normal good humor. Gene, as we were unloading Bob's boat so we could lift it out of his pickup and put it in the water, had grabbed Mike's cot and pointed to several large holes that had been burned into the fabric. Bob and Mike exchanged glances. They had been planning to save this story for around tonight's campfire but after Gene's discovery they could not wait any longer, they just had to let it out.

It started last winter when Mike was helping Bob cut firewood. As they were finishing one particularly large log, they discovered that the butt end of the old oak was hollow. They realized that it would make a tremendous chimney log and saved it back for this year's float. Luckily, they had remembered this when they were loading the boat and before leaving retrieved this gem from the woodpile. About thirty miles down the road; Mike suggested to Bob that he pull over because smoke was trailing out the bed of the truck. Bob and Mike are both smokers so they can't say for sure whose ashes from a lighted cigarette landed in the back of the truck. Of course, if your vehicle is on fire it is natural to want to stop but when they did, they discovered a basic fire fact. The high wind of the fast moving pickup suppressed the flames. When they stopped, several items in back burst into flames. The most noticeable of these was the synthetic fabric of Mike's cot. Mike pulled the cot from the truck bed and Bob suggested the fastest way to put out the fire was to pee on it. Since it was Mike's cot he vetoed that idea. (I have to mention at this time that my father once put a fire out on a grain combine by peeing on it—but that is a different story and will have to wait for another time.) Anyway, Mike reached into his cooler and pulled out a handful of ice and rubbed the flames out. While Mike was busy with his cot, Bob snuffed out several smaller fires. Further evaluation indicated that there was only one fire still underway and it was the chimney log. They threw the log onto the side of the gravel road and discussed what to do. Since this was just the beginning of a three day outing there was considerable hesitation to use up any more ice or drinking water to put out the fire. So the subject of urine came back up. Both made their best contribution. After looking at the urine soaked log still fitfully producing some tiny wisps of smoke, they had to admit most of its charm was gone. With some sadness, they got into the truck and drove off. They left the log on the side of the road with the hope that some other chimney log lover might come along and take it home.

After hearing about the chimney log transport mishap, we got the boats loaded and started downstream. It was warm for October and the day was getting progressively cloudier. By 5 PM, the sky began to suggest we'd have rain so it seemed wise not to postpone choosing a campsite. We stopped at what would be a small island during higher water levels. Firewood was plentiful and near the gravel bar where the boats were pulled up, the ground quickly rose to a higher level. If it did rain we hoped this higher gravelly area would help us avoid a muddy campsite. The only problem in the immediate vicinity was that the brush on part of the island had been cut with a tractor and rotary mower. As a matter of fact, in a field about 300 yards away we could see a farmer mowing his pasture. As the others continued to evaluate the campsite, I decided to check out our neighbor. I walked across our small island, clambered down and then up the sides of a steep gully, that would have under wetter conditions, been the second channel of the river. At the edge of this gully was a barbed wire fence that enclosed the field the farmer was mowing. As I stepped across the fence and into the open, I was surprised when I spotted three tents about 50 yards to my left. As I turned that direction, a small brown car pulled out from near the tents. I waved vigorously but in a friendly manner and the car changed its initial direction and pulled over to me. As the driver approached he partially rolled down his window and after we both said hello, he said to me, "Har yew ha disgoffer?"

As he peered into my face, I'm sure he saw a gapped-mouth, blank expression. He repeated, "Har yew ha disgoffer?" I was convinced at this point he was speaking to me in German, so I began searching the deep recesses of my mind for the few German words and phrases I know, hoping to translate his question. My mouth was just beginning to form, "No sprecken zie Duetsch", when he decided to give up on verbal communication and pointed into the middle of the field where I saw a metal pole decorated with chains and a metal basket. He made a flinging gesture and said, "Yew know—disk golf!"

Oh—disk golf—Frisbee! After a short conversation that took place entirely in English, I learned that I had arrived at the early stages of a Frisbee convention. It seems that annually disk golf devotees descend on this backwoods bourn for a weekend of flinging and flipping. I noticed that as the conversation progressed he slowly eased the window back up. I suppose my blank expression combined with my muddy boots and camouflage jacket made him begin to fear that he was in the presence of a local hillbilly/murderer. As he prepared to drive off, I decided to encourage his discomfort by telling him there were six of us, we were going to be camping on that nearby island and if he heard any whooping or yelling over there not to worry. He sped off.

When I returned to the group, they had finished surveying the island and had pronounced it suitable for our needs. As the boats were unloaded and the firewood pile grew there came an announcement from the other side of the island that a chimney log had been found. As I continued setting up camp, the others rushed off in the direction of the announcing voice and within ten minutes they returned to camp rolling the hollow butt end of a tree that was about three feet in diameter and two feet tall. This short log had been chain-sawed off square on both ends and after some final grunting it was rolled near the fire and then tipped upright on its base where it sat like a squatting missionary waiting to be sacrificed on some pagan wild-men's fire. I was glad I had warned the disk golfers about whooping and yelling.

Official happy hour began and we reviewed the day's activities. This was our second time on this part of the Gasconade River. We had floated it a few years back and each of us had to admit that no landmarks seemed familiar. This started a debate. Was the river so different after just a few years or were our mental faculties so poor? If the number of commercials on television is any indication, the most common medical condition faced by middle-aged men is something called "E. D.". In my opinion, a more widespread condition is Middle-Aged Mental Fuzziness. Since we had all been on this river just a few years ago and nothing seemed familiar, it was clear to me that we all were suffering from MAMF. This was emphasized when I opened a jar of pickled okra as a pre-supper snack, Paul bit into one and expressed delight, making some comment that he'd never tasted one before! Everyone else knew that I had been bringing the spicy little treats for at least five years and he certainly was not a pickled okra virgin. Since Paul is the oldest of our group this gave us the opportunity to torment him for his "senior moment". Wait—I hear the voice-over on the commercial now, "...it is a common condition affecting millions of men his age. With just one daily pill, Paul need not suffer any longer. Now that MAMF has been diagnosed, he will not be embarrassed by his dysfunction any longer...consult your physician before taking any medications...side affects may include excessive drooling, dry mouth, diarrhea or constipation..."

Drinks and snacks were followed by our traditional steak dinner. Just as we were finishing up supper, a gentle rain started. We all donned our rain gear and stoked up the fire. It never really rained hard so we didn't have any problem keeping the fire going but due to the soft, closed-in feeling brought on by the drizzle, the guys began to drift off to their dry beds in the tents earlier than usual.

As long as you have a quality tent, camping in a gentle rain is lovely. There is a special coziness about being secure in your bed while Mother Nature taps, taps, taps out a quiet lullaby around you. I find it particularly enjoyable because I'm one of the few of our group that does not routinely rise during the night to respond to that other water related call of nature. Over the years, on the few times that I felt I must rise, it is not unpleasant if it is a clear night. Once the decision is made, it is just a matter of quickly pulling on my coat and shoes and stepping out into the cold, crisp night. Spending some solitary time with a couple million stars can be invigorating. Hearing the gentle snoring of nearby friends makes the camp seem homey. But when it is raining and that necessity cannot be ignored, I am more likely to feel that I am being pried from the bed of my lover. That night after I had been forced by my bladder to venture out, several other times I heard the tent flaps being unzipped. This was followed by soggy steps as sleepy men also made their way to the edge of the camp.

The rain stopped during the night and I awoke to the sounds of advice being given to Mike as he searched about for dry twigs to relight the fire. I could tell by the comments being made that they were having some difficulty. I glanced at the other two bed rolls to discover I was the only one in our tent not already up. I rolled out of my bed and pulled some newspaper out of one of the two cardboard boxes stashed under my bed. I always use newspaper lined cardboard boxes to store our food. With a plastic bottle of frozen water for cooling, they work well and when empty can be tossed on the fire.

I handed the newspaper out of the tent. Mike took it to use as dry kindling. Within a few minutes, I heard the crackle of a fire underway. I could also hear the sounds of the coffee percolator being prepared for its task. I'm usually the last to get out of bed on these floating trips. Since I remove my regular clothing to sleep, unlike the others who can roll out of bed, pull on their boots and are ready to face the day, I have to get dressed. This is best done in an empty tent because it involves hopping around on one foot and first thing in the morning this could be dangerous to anyone else still lying about. I also take this time to do some minor scrubbing because even though we're "roughing it", for me a well washed face is essential to getting started in the morning.

The morning was foggy and damp but since we had chosen our camp well, we did not have too much mud to deal with. I checked my boat and saw that the back was filled up with water to the point that the batteries were submerged so I spent some time bailing. By the time I finished, the coffee was ready and I joined the others around the fire. The rest of our time was spent in our regular routine of visiting, drinking coffee and enjoying country ham and egg burritos. We slowly packed up and by 10:30 were on the water. There was some discussion to load the chimney log on the front of Gene's boat but we wisely decided that it was too heavy. So for the second time this trip, a prime chimney log was left behind. As I glanced back at the old stump still sitting next to the burned out remains of the fire, I thought I sensed a feeling of relief from the old boy. He had escaped the pagan's fire!

The next 29 hours on the river I would describe as typical—meaning wonderful. The weather was cold but lovely and the scenery was grand. The fishing was fair and the friendship was excellent. Special mention must be made of our campsite the second night. It was on a level gravel bar at the lower end of an island. We pitched the tents next to a small babbling channel on the backside of the island. It had to be the most picturesque location we had ever visited. Several times during the night we heard the sharp splash of a nearby beaver slapping his tail on the water in anger over having to share his beautiful home with humans.

As I said, the float proceeded in a typical manner until Saturday afternoon. When we begin to realize that we are only a couple of miles from the take-out we often slow down, put our fishing poles away and join the boats together and float as a group along the slow stretches of the river. This allows us to savor the last couple of hours of our annual trip together. It is necessary from time to time to separate and run the narrow places or small "rapids" that appear. As a rule, we always have Gene bring up the rear because he has a gasoline powered outboard motor and more than once on these trips one or more of the boats has run out of battery power some miles short of the boat ramp.

I should mention that Saturday morning Bob had decided to join Gene in his boat, turning his boat over to Mike and Paul. At about three o'clock we observed a narrowing of the river ahead and decided to separate for our individual runs. This was not a typical shallow area but a severe restriction where the entire force of the river was concentrated in narrow deep channel where the river was rapidly undercutting a tree covered bank. The outside of the curving bend was a tumble of downed trees submerged in roiling and churning water. Russ and I passed easily through the most treacherous part and except for ducking some low hanging branches near the end of the run had no difficulty. As each boat hesitates at the top of such a rapid area and then moves on through, the boats tend to get separated. We were probably a quarter of a mile downstream before we were joined by Mike and Paul who had a similar experience. We continued our quiet float together until a comment from Mike made us turn our attention back upstream. He was the only one still watching for Gene and Bob and he noticed something unusual. Way upstream something red, white and rectangular had just come around the bend. Could it be a floating cooler? We discussed this for a couple of seconds. Russ got out his binoculars. By the time he focused on the object, a white bucket appeared. Flotsam! Something must be wrong. We turned the boats around and slowly began to head upstream.

Our small trolling motors have never been too efficient at moving upstream. And it seemed to take a long time to approach the low end of the rapids. All during this time we saw more and more floating items. And since no boat, Bob or Gene had appeared I was beginning to get anxious.

Mike decided our progress was too slow so he and Paul pulled over to run along the bank. They disappeared around the bend. We were given the task to collect the floating items. I have to admit I was glad to have that job. I've seen canoes crushed by the power of a river and heard stories of drowning caused by overturned boats. If Russ, in the front of my boat, was having the same thoughts he likewise was keeping them to himself. At this point we had collected a cooler, two buckets and a life jacket. We began to circle about after smaller items like an empty beer can and a floating Planter's peanut can when we heard a call from Mike, "Are you all right?" We held our breath for a response. Nothing. Russ called out, "Are they all right?" Mike called back, "Yeah, they're OK."

Eventually the current became too swift for us to make any upstream progress and we pulled to shore to walk the remaining distance. I was shocked when I rounded the bend. Gene's boat was completely submerged except for one small rear corner. The force of the current was crushing it against some downed trees. Gene and Bob were still wading about in the swift water, slowly removing items from the boat and transferring them to the shore. By this time both of them had been soaked to the skin for at least 40 minutes. Mike, calculating that the water temperature was probably in the low fifties and the air temperature was in the high forties, noted that

Bob was shivering uncontrollably—a sign of hypothermia—and insisted he get out of the water and into dry clothes. They went off to build a fire in a sheltered area as the rest of us tried to coax Gene out of the water. He was in what I call "crazed farmer mode". A pattern of behavior all of us are familiar with, having seen livestock crash through fences, hay wagons unload themselves on busy highways and combines get stuck irretrievably in the mud. We finally got him out long enough to have a serious conversation about how to proceed. He was convinced that the boat was not going to budge because he and Bob had pushed on it with all their strength. Just as we were trying to come up with plan B, a jet powered gigging boat came from upstream. Driving was a big guy with a long white beard in bib overalls. With him were his wife, daughter and son-in-law. We had waved to them a couple of hours earlier when we met them going upstream. Gene and Paul asked them if they could help us. Russ and I walked upstream where the river could be waded and crossed to retrieve all the equipment that had been removed from the boat by Gene and Bob and piled on the other side. We were busy at that task for quite a while because it was not easy wading across carrying all the water soaked equipment. While we were there, Mike helped Bob change into dry clothes near the smoking fire. At one point we stopped to watch our Good Samaritan slowly maneuver his boat towards Gene's from downstream in an attempt to tie on and pull it free. They tried without success and within moments he was swept downstream where his boat's stern pushed up on a sunken tree. It lurched wildly, not tipping over only because Gene, having also been swept along with the boat, was in the water struggling to hold the bow level. We watched anxiously as the boat's owner partially stepped from his boat onto a downed tree and tried to rock his boat free. I was certain that at any moment we would have two sunken boats in the river. After several minutes of hard work they broke it free but then the boat spun wildly in the river and was pushed stern first into a gravel bar. At this point the engine would not restart. Eventually, it was determined a piece of gravel was jammed into the jet prop. They spent several minutes working to get the rock out and the boat started and then they wisely decided not to make a second attempt. Russ and I were finished moving equipment. Bob and Mike had returned from the fire and Gene and Paul joined us on the gravel bar straight across from the sunken boat and we decided we needed a plan C.

Gene was still in his wet clothes so he waded out to his boat with a couple lengths of rope we had tied together. We hoped that if we could shift the boat sideways maybe the current would help push it off the submerged trees. He tied the rope on the front corner and as he pushed we all lined up and pulled on the rope. Since I was wet up to the knees I was in front of the line partially out into the stream. With Gene pushing with all his might and all of us pulling, I saw the boat shift slightly. Just then the rope broke and we all went tumbling. Fortunately no one was hurt as we collapsed on top of each other. One of the ropes was rotten and had pulled apart under the strain. Since I was convinced I had seen the boat shift I encouraged us to try again. A second pull with everyone bracing themselves for another snapped rope pulled the boat slightly downstream where the current spun the boat around and then free.

Once we pulled the boat to shore and tipped it over to pour out the water we began to move quickly. It was approaching 6 PM and the light was fading fast. Gene went over to the fire to change into dry clothes and we reloaded his boat. Shortly we were on the water again and Gene and Bob told the story of their disaster. Their misfortune started when Bob, after observing the unusually fast water the two boats ahead of him had just passed through, uttered the following words, "I'm glad this boat can't tip over." At the time that may not have seemed foolish because we had always viewed Gene's boat as the large, stable craft of our expedition. But in retrospect any such comment has to be viewed as similar to the design engineer of the Titanic saying his ship cannot sink! Such statements have to be viewed as hubris or at the very least ignorance by Poseidon or whatever lesser river god may be listening. In either case they were most likely doomed from that point on. About halfway through the bend, the front of the boat ran up on a partially sunken tree. With Bob riding the reared-up front of the boat like a cowboy riding a horse standing on its hind legs, Gene turned to discover water pouring in over the stern. The boat sank quickly. As the boat went down Bob leaped out and had a brief scare when he hit the water and one leg got temporarily tangled in sunken branches. They climbed out on opposite sides of the river and had a few additional anxious moments when they each feared the other may still be in the water. They then waded back out to retrieve what they could from the boat and that was how Mike and Paul found them.

Once we were moving downstream again we came up to the gigging boat that had tried to help us. At this point it was dark and we asked them how far we were from the boat ramp because we had some fear we might go past it. They said it was about a mile ahead and there was a light in the parking lot so we could not miss it. They had their big gigging light going and were trying to spear a late supper. Without saying a word to us they turned their boat around and began slowly moving downriver. They acted like they were still gigging but we realized they were actually guiding us along. We were pleased to have the help because this section of the river was full of large sunken rocks and downed driftwood. After helping us through this treacherous section they told us the boat ramp was about half a mile ahead and turned around to continue their pursuit.

We had traveled through that section with the rocks and snags single file. Gene and Bob were in the lead but Russ and I soon overtook them. Fortunately, Gene's trolling motor had not been damaged by being completely submerged. He had simply turned it upside down, poured the water out and it worked. He lost his batteries in the crash and so had taken one of mine. The problem was that it was nearly drained of electricity. It was now failing and as we pulled alongside we grabbed their boat to give them a tow. I was anxious to get to the boat ramp and proceeded on expecting Paul and Mike to overtake us now that I was pushing two boats. When they did not appear we slowed down and eventually heard the occasional "clunk" of paddles against the side of a boat. Shortly, they appeared out of the nighttime gloom. Their tired battery had died and so they had resorted to manpower. We held the three boats together and my motor slowly moved us downstream. We believed we must be close to the take-out but no parking lot light was visible. We continued on for another quarter mile. There was talk of the possibility of missing the boat ramp in the darkness and floating endlessly past it. Somewhere Gene came up with a feeble flashlight and began to scan the left bank for a boat ramp. I could tell by the quiet change in pitch of the hum from my trolling motor that my battery was down to its last few thousand electrons. All eyes were on the pale sweep of flashlight along the shore. Suddenly a white strip glowed in the darkness— the boat ramp! All hands grabbed paddles and within a few minutes we were on terra firma.

I'm sure all of us were fairly stressed-out by the time our feet touched the boat ramp. I felt pretty good about the whole thing and basically considered it quite an adventure. This was due mostly to the fact that no one had been injured and it was Gene's boat, not mine, that had been underwater. Our day wasn't completely done; we still had to shuttle back up to the put-in to get our vehicles and then drive home. During this time, I realized it may take each of us a different amount of time to come to grips with our adventure. I know it happened for Paul a couple of hours later. We were standing around the trucks preparing the last few items for the drive up the gravel road away from the river. From the darkness we heard him pop a beer, take a swig, let out a long, deep sigh and in a nearly inaudible voice say, "Shee—it".

CHAPTER EIGHT

The Salvage Operation

We were relieved that no one had been injured as a result of Gene's boat sinking. It was so late by the time we got off the river and we were in such a hurry to get home that we really hadn't taken time to inventory the items that had sunk to the bottom of the river. During the next several days, by email, a list began to form; three trolling motor batteries, a tackle box, two fishing poles, a folding camp chair, a sleeping mat, a small sack of camp equipment and a maroon canvas bag. This maroon bag contained, a well balanced hatchet, a strong little barbeque grill, a medium sized, enamel metal cook pot and an extra large, well seasoned, cast iron skillet. I suspect that you can tell by my use of adjectives, which of these lost items were of personal importance to me. So upon our return, the great sinking story was told and retold in six different households. With each telling of my own version, the wistful expressions about the maroon bag and its contents became more intense. Certain questions began to form in my mind. Wasn't the water this year unusually clear? How far would various objects tumble in the current before hitting bottom? Could a long wooden pole with a metal hook on the end snag these waiting items? Was it possible for my boat with my little trolling motor to navigate the shallows and snags to return to the crash site? Hmm…It might be fun to try. It might be a good excuse to get my boat out on the water one last time this year. It might make a good story to tell the other White Trash River Boys. And, I might get my skillet back.

I called a couple of the boys and I didn't get a strong sense of support for the idea. Various excuses were made all due to family obligations. As my brother Paul has jokingly said when we are attempting to choose the best dates to fit everyone's calendar for our annual float, "Don't these guys know that floating and fishing take priority over family?" While family may have been the reason voiced for their inability to come, I began to suspect that the cold water and fast current had taken the edge off these guys' interest. That created a problem for me because there was no doubt that I needed a copilot for this adventure. He'd have to be the lookout and hookman in the front of the boat while I ran the motor from the rear. It didn't take long to realize that my friend Roy would do quite well. Roy, an avid outdoorsman and on at least one occasion a substitute White Trash River Boy, responded that he was ready to take up the challenge.

We all know that everyone complains about the weather but no one does anything about it. In Missouri, the complaints are divided between long, humid summers or long, cloudy winters. "Hot enough for ya? Cold enough for ya? All that might be true but I respond with unreserved enthusiasm for October; bright days, blue-blue skies, crisp mornings with warm afternoons and advancing fall colors. Uncharacteristically, this year we had been cheated. The drizzly, cold days that had accompanied us during our float trip had been typical for the entire month. Now it was the second week of November and the forecast was for more rain for Friday and Saturday. Roy disappointed me when he suggested we hold off making final plans unless the weather opened up. I thought to myself, "Man, can't I find anyone who understands how important it is to get my skillet back?" Oops, check that—I shouldn't care so much for a skillet—I have to remember I'm in this for the adventure, I don't want to appear overly attached to cookware and the actual chances for finding it are quite slim. Anyway, late in the week the weather opened up and we were on our way Friday afternoon.

It's about an hour and a half drive to the Paydown Access on the Gasconade River. On the way we made a short diversionary stop at

Hilkemeyer's, a hunting-fishing-trapping-boating-partial museum-convenience store. They had a brand new version of my cast iron skillet for $14.95. A very reasonable price, with the understanding that a new cast iron skillet can never compete with a well used one. I commented to Roy that if we failed in our retrieval attempt, we'd stop on our way back to buy it.

We were the only vehicle in the river access parking lot when we pulled in. I backed down the ramp, we quickly unloaded the boat from my truck and then I pulled over to a slightly secluded area where we staked a claim to the best camping site. Moments later a second pickup and boat pulled in and repeated the process but they had to choose to camp next to the outhouses. This was a good sign.

We loaded in the boat our fishing equipment, coolers and a long pole with a sturdy hook attached to its end that I had made up just for this operation. We shoved off. I don't know if Roy was surprised or not but I made no pretense to start fishing. I headed up stream to the crash site. I knew of the rocks and snags ahead so I sternly warned Roy that it was his responsibility to not let me rip the propeller off on a sunken tree or rock. He sat forward in his seat and took on his task in a good-natured and serious manner.

It took about an hour to run through one series of sunken snags, past two shallow gravel areas and one minefield of barely sunken boulders.

This took us to the broad deep area just below the crash site where Russ and I had spent our time fishing floating objects from the river while Paul and Mike had continued upstream to rescue our fallen comrades. Now, Roy was sitting on the seat at the bow of the boat and I encouraged him to grab the pole and begin to scan the bottom for treasure. Just a few moments later, Roy announced that he spotted a five-gallon white plastic bucket on the bottom. I also caught a glimpse of it as we passed so I circled around and encouraged Roy to prepare to hook it, stating that the boys often pack camping items in just those types of buckets. We pulled up to the bucket and I dropped back to the second slowest speed so we could remain nearly stationary in the current. Roy began to grapple with the bucket, rolling it around on the river bottom until he could get the hook on the wire bail handle. A final effort was necessary to lift the bucket into the boat because being full of water it weighed over fifty pounds. I was chattering excitedly about our first recovery when I observed that the expression on Roy's face didn't match my enthusiasm. I began to express my surprise about the amount of moss that could grow on a plastic bucket in just under two weeks when the boat rotated in the current and I faced into the day's steady breeze. Immediately, the cause for Roy's expression wafted across my end of the boat. "Yikes!" I said, "Is that smell coming from that bucket?" Roy with his horizontal lips pressed firmly together nodded an affirmation. Still slightly confused by this rapid turn of events, I was preparing to suggest we take off the top of the bucket to see what was inside but I could not make my mouth form the words. Roy appeared to be reading my mind and had ever so slightly backed away from the bucket. By raising both his palms towards the offensive object, in an attempt to ward off the stench, he made it clear he would have nothing more to do with our discovery. I mumbled something about our guys having a bucket full of nothing that could smell that bad. Then I pulled myself together and with a voice a half of an octave higher than usual said, "Throw it back in the river!" Roy who had at this point moved as far forward in the bow as was possible without actually abandoning ship seemed to hesitate to follow captain's orders. I voiced an even higher version of "Throw it back in the river!" and likely included some odor adjectives just in case he was partially stunned by smell. Squeezing his lips even more tightly together he quickly pitched it overboard. So much for our first find!

With a fresh breeze blowing in our face, we again pointed the boat upstream. Clearly, we had brought up some bucket full of rotten fish bait used to chum the river for catfish or other bottom feeding species. We could have had a long laugh about it but Roy who was still scanning the bottom quickly announced he saw a fishing pole. At least the chum bucket had been good training. With just a few moments effort one of Bob's fishing poles, or should I say, the bottom half of a pole was in the boat. As we slowly approached the crash site we eventually found that we could make no headway as the current began to out-muscle the trolling motor. We pulled over to the gravel bar to access the situation. We walked up to the crash site. The current was way too strong to search in that area with my little motor but we both agreed there was an area just below that we had not completely searched. So we returned to the boat and by varying the motor's speed I could hold us nearly stationary in the water while Roy scanned the bottom. Within minutes he had spotted something green and after some mighty struggling pulled a water-filled bag containing a folding camp chair into the boat. Another great find! My confidence began to rise to the expectation that we might recover all sorts of treasure. In my enthusiasm to search this area and maintain control of the boat against the rushing water, I suddenly realized that I had positioned the boat near some sunken trees that were very similar to the ones that had caused Gene's disaster. Roy was intently bent over his job and from time to time encouraged me to the left or right. As those treacherous branches loomed near my stern I began to feel my blood pressure rise. I feared we were loosing the battle with the current and were being swept backwards towards those snags; I called to Roy to grab a paddle and help us get to the left bank. With his powerful pulls, we quickly were safe and standing on the gravel bar.

We agreed that we had searched the area below the crash site quite extensively and had made no additional finds. Roy began to describe complex maneuvers that I could perform with the boat to hold us over the crash site while he searched. I vetoed any actions that would place the boat directly above the scary snags. We began to feel stymied until Roy suggested that I stand on an upper gravel bar and let the boat, by the rope, down into the danger area. I suggested I could do one better and began to strip off my shoes, socks and pants, stating that I was willing to wade into the stream and hold the boat in position. As I put my shoes back on, I did include one caveat, stating that a couple of important parts of my anatomy just below my waist were not going to be dipped into the frigid water. So, I held onto the front of the boat and allowed it to swing in the current as I pushed Roy, poised in the stern with the long pole, over the crash site. Due to the strong current, I could only make the boat scribe long arcs over the area we were searching before I would pull it back upstream to make another attempt. A mysterious whitish, square object was seen but although Roy could move it with the pole he could not hook it. A short length of PVC pipe (a fishing accessory from Gene's boat) was retrieved. Once Roy caused me considerable excitement when he stated he saw something that resembled the maroon bag on the bottom but after attempting to hook it on the second pass it turned out to be a pile of sunken leaves. After any futile pass over the bottom, Roy would exhort me to push the boat a little farther into the stream. At one point I announced that my new maximum level of immersion was my nipples because my privates had been flash frozen several minutes earlier. Now that they were intensely shrunken, it didn't seem to matter anymore.

After about another twenty minutes our number of retrievals seemed to have stalled. I looked at my watch and since it was five o'clock it was time to begin the return journey to the boat ramp. That would give us thirty minutes of good light for the trip. Before I stepped into the boat I spotted an empty bottle on the gravel bar, Peach Brandy. I recalled that before the crash, the two sunken boaters had been seen making a valiant attempt to empty just such a bottle. I collected it and marked it People's Exhibit #1. If, at next year's float, the two victims begin to weave a tale of excessive self-promotion the bottle may become important evidence.

The return to camp was uneventful. Although well soaked, I did not begin uncontrollably shivering until I was back at camp. A dry change of clothes and a fire quickly kindled by Roy immediately warmed me up. An enjoyable evening was spent by the campfire which included a delicious steak dinner. I slept like a baby. Roy, forgetting his cot, spent part of the night fighting various rocks but for a guy who claims not to snore, I have to say I was glad I had my ear plugs. Hot coffee, bacon, eggs and raisin toast started our morning. We spent the day fishing with some limited success and by 3 PM we were off the river and on the way home. Within a half hour, we were pushing on the locked door at Hilkemeyer's Store. "Closed", the sign said. "Guess I won't be buying a skillet here today!"

Back home we divided our camping equipment and Roy headed down the driveway to his house. I asked Janet, my wife, to take a picture of me with the recovered booty. As we stood in the rapidly dimming evening light, I regaled her with the tale of our adventure. Of course, she asked about the skillet and other cooking accoutrements. "No luck," I said sadly. "I didn't even have any luck buying a new one."

"Let's go in the house." She said as she led me through the front door. "You'll feel better once you're inside." Assuming she was referring to a hot shower, I was stunned as I walked in to see my maroon bag in the center of the hall. I knelt quickly and zipped it open. A well balanced hatchet, a strong little barbeque grill, a medium sized, enamel metal cook pot and an extra large, well seasoned, cast iron skillet—all inside. Janet said that Gene had brought it over last night. He also had one of the missing fishing poles. She said I was to call Gene to get the complete story.

A few minutes later I was on the phone and Gene was telling me his story. "I got a letter in the mail a few days ago. It was from a guy in Belle, Missouri who had found my tackle box, your cooking stuff and the pole in the river."

"Who was this guy? How did he know it was our stuff he found?" I asked.

"He found my fishing license inside my tackle box. He tried to call me but my name was misspelled on the license so after not finding me in the phone book he sent me a letter. He gigs on the river and was with the group that was camped on the gravel bar just below where we got in trouble. He went up there at night and with his gigging lights could see a lot of our stuff on the bottom. This was the stuff he could get a hold of with his gig. After I got the letter I gave him a call. He said he was going to be at the Pizza Hut in Jefferson City that evening and if I wanted to meet him there he'd have my gear. I drove right down and you know what? He had taken out all the tackle and cleaned and oiled it. He washed out your duffle bag and cleaned, dried and oiled your cooking stuff. I tried to give him twenty bucks but he wouldn't take it. He said he spent a lot of time on the river and the right thing to do was just help anyone he could along the way."

Over the past twelve years we have had some adventures and some misadventures but what has been most important to us is the rare opportunity to enjoy two slow, nature-filled days in manly companionship. And yes, this particular autumn provided us with stories and memories that will be enjoyed over the next many seasons. Upon reflection one thought, I'm sure, will return again and again. It is simply, thank God, the Great Mystery, Fate, the River Spirit or what ever name you wish to call The One, for keeping track of all things great and small—right down to making sure that Hilkemeyer's Store was closed so that I didn't end up with two skillets.

CHAPTER NINE

River Fishing

While I take considerable pride in my camp prepared meals, I have to admit that I am not a fishing powerhouse. From the very beginning of our White Trash adventures, the second night's entrée is fish. Thankfully, the other five members of our group can be counted on to make their contribution to that meal. There are many different techniques to put fish in the frying pan. The following brief comments are just to give you an overview of the methods that we have enjoyed. If you want detailed training you should consult a fishing techniques book, a fishing website, a sales clerk at your local sporting supply store or best of all find someone to take you fishing. Be sure to get a state fishing license and obey all fishing regulations for each of the methods described below.

Bass Fishing
We spend most of our time fishing for bass. Most of us use a 5-6' rod with a spinner type

reel. I can't begin to describe all the different types of plastic worms, grubs and hard lures we use. We have tried live bait in the past and the artificial lures seem more effective. As we drift downriver we fish areas where the water is not too swift or too slow and we pay special attention to sunken trees and rocks usually on the deeper side of the river. We generally keep moving with the current, so that means that we rarely get more than one cast into any single spot. Usually the person in the back of the boat will be attracted to the same spot and cast there also. If an area has slow water immediately adjacent to the main, fast current and also has obstructions where the fish can hide, one of the boats will linger there and fish that location hard. Rarely do the three boats fish closely together but most of the time we remain in sight of each other. It has been our experience that the best bass fishing in October, when we are on the river, is before 10 AM and after 4 PM. We know this but rarely are we on the river much before ten or more than hour or an hour and a half after four. Many times we have been concerned that supper is going to be skimpy and while the first two boats are choosing and setting up the campsite the last boat finally arrives with a mess of fish to make supper bountiful.

Crappie Fishing

Crappie fishing uses the same equipment as bass but with smaller lures. Small feather covered lures (I grew up calling them "doll-flies") work well. We tend to find crappie in slightly slower, slightly deeper water than where the bass are located.

Catfish Fishing

In Italy, if all roads lead to Rome, then in central Missouri all streams lead to the Mighty Mo. During the years that we float sections near the Missouri we pay more attention to the big boys of river fish—the cats. Using a rod and reel for catfish means putting on a treble hook about three feet below a fairly heavy lead sinker. Most catfish baits are not for the squeamish. A variety of stink baits and dough balls are available in jars at your sporting goods store. Raw chicken liver is probably the best for this method because it stays on the hook. Strangely enough, a treble hook baited with canned corn can also be effective. The cats are usually located in the deep, broad, slow areas of the river. We allow the line to play out behind the boat as we drift through these slower areas called "chutes".

Trot Lines

A variety of fish can be caught on trot, limb and jug lines using the same baits described above for catfish, with the primary target still being catfish. Additional bait is live gold fish that can be purchased at a bait shop. Trot lines involve the purchase of a long length of heavy nylon string that is rigged with baited treble hooks. These hooks dangle at regular intervals on short lengths of string. One end of the long string is tied to a partially sunken log or some other stable object and the other end to a rock or brick sunken downstream. This causes the baited line to be strung out in the river. Ideally the line should be checked once or twice during the night to see if anything has been caught.

Jug Lines

Jug lines are a lot of fun on the river. About a 3' length of trot line type cord is tied on the handle of an empty laundry bleach jug, a treble hook tied on the other end and then baited and the rig is tossed in the river before you shove off in the morning. The less White Trash method is to make special floats out of brightly colored floating plastic. As you progress down the river you collect the floating jugs. If you are lucky, you remove any caught fish.

Limb Lines

Limb lines are lengths of trot line type cord with a baited treble hook on one end and the other end tied on a convenient tree branch that hangs over the river. A number of these are put out and checked once or twice during the night.

Bank Sets

Gene is our bank set specialist. About a half hour before dark he baits his rod and reel as he would for river fishing catfish. While standing on the riverbank near our campsite he casts the line in the water and lets it float downstream. He then sticks the handle end of the rod into the river bank, props up the tip of the rod with a forked stick, attaches a bell to the end of the rod and then joins us at the fire. For the couple of hours while we drink beer, eat supper and visit around the fire we are continually amused as Gene, the only one listening for the gentle tinkling of a distant bell, will suddenly spring to his feet, leap any objects in his direct path to the river and disappear into the darkness. Usually he returns and morosely states that the fish broke the line, or in some other manner got the bait off the hook without getting itself caught but about one out of three times he announces that he's caught a nice catfish. Many times while I am frying our meager assortment of bass and crappie, fresh catfish fillets, caught by Gene using this method, appear just in the nick of time to augment our supper.

Gigging

Gigging is not fishing in the traditional sense. It can more properly be thought of as stalking and spearing fish. It is a time honored tradition. I have a 150 year old lithograph on my wall of an American Indian standing in a canoe holding his spear at the ready. Dangling from the front of the boat is some sort of flaming basket. Modern giggers have specially designed boats propelled by jet outboard motors. Huge generator powered electric lights sit on the front below a railing where two giggers stand. Their prey is what is called non-game fish—carp, red horse and suckers. Ugly fish that when properly deep fried can make an excellent meal. I have to admit that we have not tried gigging yet but I have a spotlight that runs off a trolling battery and Gene has a gig so it is only a matter of time before we get both of these items at the river during the same year and we can try gigging White Trash River Boy style.

<u>Cleaning Fish</u>

If you catch fish and want to eat them, then you will have to clean fish. Mike always takes the lead in this task and it is too complex of a topic to cover here except to suggest that at the campfire any fish recipe should start with boneless, skinless fillets.

CHAPTER TEN

Still White Trash

One Saturday afternoon the summer before last I was out running an errand. On the way home I did something very unusual for me, I stopped at a garage sale. I don't believe in buying other people's junk but I must have had a moment of weakness because I stopped. After making a quick circle through the tables and then remembering why I don't stop at garage sales, I turned and headed back down the driveway. A voice from the cool shadows of a garage called to me. "You're not interested in buying a boat are you?" I stopped in mid-stride and half turned to the hidden voice. In that instant, a repressed event passed through my brain. Russ and I were tied up to the bank on the Gasconade River in my overloaded aluminum row boat. The V-shaped bow was piled full of camping and fishing equipment and I was in the stern. Russ was standing on the bank preparing to push us into the current. Russ had several years practice developing his technique. First, he would ask me if I was ready to go. This meant I was to sit down and grasp the boat's gunwales. Next, he would make sure he had his left foot securely placed on the edge of the muddy river bank. Then with one swift, smooth motion he would push the boat off, take a giant step, vault over all the camping and fishing stuff, pirouette on his right foot as it lightly touched the one small clearing left open just in front of his seat and then land his butt squarely in the folding chair that served as his seat. Over a ten-plus-year period he had probably performed this feat over one hundred times. This time something went wrong. His right foot missed the one small clearing and began to descend on his tackle box. Wanting to avoid crushing all his gear he tried an airborne pirouette. Now, the always tippy bow of the boat began to react to these gyrations and like a skittish horse moved out from under Russ. As he came down on the side of the boat for a moment it seemed that we would capsize. I leaned hard the opposite direction and Russ realizing that he was a goner slipped over the side. He went in and to my surprise all the way under. When his head resurfaced, he announced he was unhurt. I rarely take pleasure in other's misfortune but I'll admit to laughing heartily when he was safely in the boat.

The day Russ got dunked was probably the day I began to subconsciously look for a different boat. The other boys had always used jon boats and I had grown to admire their stability. A few years ago Gene purchased his boat and so I had more reason to fault the qualities of my diminutive little row boat. I pride myself on being a practical minded fellow and often said that one of the basic philosophies of the White Trash River Boys is, "make due with what you have" but anyone who has ever owned a boat knows that boat owners have a wandering eye. So here I was in somebody's driveway amid garage sale items that by Saturday afternoon were clearly not going to sell, when that sultry female voice in the darkness called to me, "Hey, sailor. Want to have a good time?"

Well, actually all she had said was, "There's a jon boat in the backyard if you are interested." I went around to check it out. It clearly had not been used for years. It was sitting on the ground with a couple of sticks of firewood under the bow. This was to partially tip it up so rainwater could flow out the open drain hole in the stern. It had some rotten indoor/outdoor carpet glued on the inside and two swivel boat seats. It was 14' long— just the right size.

"How much are you asking?" I said when I returned to the garage.

"Four hundred dollars" she said. I asked a few questions. It turned out she was the daughter-in-law of the elderly couple who had passed away. The contents of the house were being sold off and that included the boat.

"If you'll take two-fifty, I'll buy it" I said. She responded that she'd have to call her husband because he was the one who had priced it. "He's not home now, so give me your number and if he says OK, I'll call you."

Three hours later I was on the phone to my neighbor and fellow White Trash River Boy, Gene, telling him I had bought a boat and asking his help to pick it up. I knew that I was not strong enough to drag the boat uphill from the backyard by myself and the back of my truck has a number of built in tool boxes so I needed Gene's truck. Within a short time, Gene drove up my driveway and he had his teenage son along. That was good—another strong back. An hour later, we had unloaded my purchase onto the lawn at the side of my house, Gene and Chase headed home and I started pulling rotten carpet from the boat.

There are two famous clichés about boats. The first is, "The two happiest days in a boat owner's life is the day he buys his boat and the day he sells his boat." The second is, "A boat is a hole in the water you pour money into." The first cliché doesn't have much meaning for me because I didn't have to sell my old row boat, I just returned it to the spot I borrowed it from. The second certainly rings true for me. If you have ever owned a boat you know that once you purchase it, you are on a slippery slope. Now that the boat was in my yard and Gene and his truck were gone, an important question came to mind.

How was I going to transport it? With all those tool boxes in my truck, I had been thinking for quite a long time that I needed a little, flat-bed trailer to haul stuff. This imaginary little trailer could be a boat trailer and a utility trailer for lumber, etc. all in one. Actually the slippery slope is the best thing about having a boat, there is always something that needs to be bought or built. Women have jewelry and clothes to use and collect, men have tools and sporting equipment.

After a winter and spring of thinking, measuring and shopping, at an Easter gathering of my wife's family, I mentioned my need for a utility trailer to my wife's nephew. I had seen several nice trailers that he had built from scratch and after a brief discussion he agreed to build me one just the right size for my boat. So by early fall I had my boat with all the former owner's carpeting and other accoutrements removed, loaded in my new trailer with all my personalized touches added to the outfit. Only one thing was missing from my wish list and that was a small outboard motor.

Outboard motors represent to me the essence of capitalism. First, they are compact, sleek powerhouses. From a technological point of view they are simply sexy. Secondly, they are in my opinion ridiculously expensive. You can buy a nice lawn mower for $400 but any kind of outboard motor is going to push $1200. The lawnmower is squat, utilitarian and a necessity to anyone who owns a yard. This is naturally going to drive the price as low as it can go. An outboard motor is none of these—so screw the fool who wants one and jack the price way up. This caused me to wonder aloud in Janet's presence if I could buy a gasoline weed whacker and put a propeller on the end to serve as an inexpensive outboard motor. She rolled her eyes and told me to go buy a dependable outboard and get over it. Still resisting the expense, I shopped extensively for used models but found them to be nearly as expensive as new. Searching the Internet and e-Bay didn't turn up any bargains either. Eventually I found a dealer in St. Louis with a brand new, two cylinder, 6 horse power Mercury for a good price, so I bit the bullet and bought it.

All this talk about my boat, motor and trailer has a point and it can be made by describing the most recent year of our annual float. It started when Gene pulled up in his two year old crew cab, 4x4, Ford pickup towing his three year old boat and trailer and he backed down the boat ramp. I waited my turn with my nice little boat with new outboard, new trailer and a one year old club-cab, 4x4, Chevy pickup. Bob arrived with his boat still sticking out the back of his pickup but instead of the rusted out hulk he had driven for years, he had a new, 4x4, Ram pickup. Not counting Russ' car, that we left at the take-out, we floated away leaving just under $60,000 worth of vehicles behind in the parking lot. We pulled up to the gravel bar campsite later that evening and unloaded our equipment. Now I've already mentioned our boats and I'll just make a quick mention of the nice fishing poles and tackle boxes that each of us leave in the boats as we set up camp. Camp itself looks very different than years ago. This has been a gradual change. Almost every year the first night on the river is spent showing and admiring the one or two pieces of new equipment that have been purchased or received as Christmas presents in the previous year. Nice spacious tents, comfortable cots, self-inflating air mattresses, fluffy sleeping bags all insure a good night's sleep. Folding camp chairs to sit on around the campfire, instead of beer coolers, provide good back support in the hours to come. At suppertime the menu has not changed but how it is prepared and served has. A camp table is used to help prepare the meal. This reduces the squatting and bending that was so common in the past. Dinner is served on a large table which we all gather around in our chairs. A gas lantern is placed in the middle so we can actually see what we are eating. And finally, Gene shocked us last year by asking if anyone would like some wine with the meal and then proceeded to produce a corkscrew. Of course, red wine the first night to go with the steak and white the second for the fish.

So, all this fancy equipment and fancy eating raises the question. Are we still the White Trash River Boys? Years ago, I began to call us the White Trash River Boys not because of the equipment we had but because of several fundamental beliefs. I guess you could call it a muddy boot, camouflage hunting-jacket type of philosophy.

Regardless of who we become, we will not forget where we came from. All the White Trash River Boys were raised on the farm and with that comes a love for the land. As a society most of us have farming ancestors but our modern world has become so separated from that life. We realize that our strength comes from the land. Whether it's harvesting a tomato from our garden or hunting deer in a quiet, leaf-littered forest, we are physically stronger for the experience.

Another White Trash belief is to enjoy what you have. You have not read in this book about fishing the Arctic streams in Siberia or rafting the Colorado. All the joys of life are within easy grasp, whether that be holding your wife next to you or holding your fishing rod as you cast into a local lake or stream. Grasping for something that is always bigger and better will only force you to tread a path of discontent.

And finally, we have a commitment to the greatest experience of all—to search and find God. We search for the God who is found in nature and I don't just mean the fluffy-cloud-filled-sky, tree-hugging sort of nature but also the tooth and claw nature. God is present when the wiggling fish is killed in the claws of the osprey or under the fisherman's knife. God is present in the cold autumn rain and in the warm breeze that gently blows up the hill on a spring afternoon. God is present in the solitude of snowy woods and God is present in the strong handshake of friends as they part ways on a sunny boat ramp.

Epilogue

The following is a short story I wrote a few years ago. It does not deal directly with the White Trash River Boys but I feel it captures our essential spirit. I hope you enjoy it as a small bonus.

"The Hunter"

"Paw-Hiu-Skah".

A voice poked through the darkness.

"Paw-Hiu-Skah!" The voice was more insistent this time.

"What, my love?" White Hair turned his head heavily to see the silhouette of his wife standing over him.

"The sun is almost up. You'll be late."

"Thank you, my love." He slowly rolled to his side, pushed back the heavy cover and sat upright. For the last few days, rising and getting out of bed had become particularly difficult. He pulled on a shirt and started for the door. When he reached the opening he paused and returned to the bed and removed the black buffalo blanket he had moments before been under and wrapped the warm fur around his shoulders. He stepped into the gray fog. There were no signs of frost except for a silvery sheen on a few wooden drying frames some distance from the houses. As he climbed the hill to the north of the village the air began to clear. The sky was pale blue and all the stars had disappeared except for the wandering morning star. By the time he reached his customary prayer place, even it had fled before the power of Grandfather Sun. When he had finished singing his prayers, the sun was a complete sphere. As he sat quietly his attention became focused on five deer which were moving slowly across an opening on the western ridge. He smiled at himself when he realized that he had subconsciously pursed his lips in the direction of the deer. It was a quiet gesture usually directed to other members of a hunting party to attract their attention to nearby game. But he was alone here, at least alone on this ridge now. The other men who had been out for their morning prayers were probably returning to the village. White Hair felt no urge to move. The morning was just too beautiful. Besides, he was sitting in the sun and the village below him was still covered in a snake-like wrap of fog. The warm sun seemed to force life into his tired body.

Paw-Hiu-Skah was not an old man. He considered himself in his prime of life. Yes, when he occasionally let his normally shaved hair grow, there were streaks of gray at his temples but he had carried his name—White Hair—since his youth. His dark hair in a certain light had a brilliant sheen, which made it appear to be highlighted with white dust. As a vain youth he often decorated his hair with the long fur from the tail of the white tail deer to reinforce the impression. Back then, he loved to strut for the girls. Now, he had sons of that age. He was in his middle years; not old enough to be one of the retired old bulls, who sat in the shade discussing serious matters and not young enough to be a wild panther, concerned only with hunting, warfare and the beautiful girls. He was one of adult men who held the responsibility of making sure the village survived and prospered.

In the last few months that responsibility had weighed heavily upon him. The village had just returned from the fall buffalo hunt on the western prairie. He had been in charge, for the fifth year now, of the drive and hunt. It is probably the single most important activity the village engages in for the year. Each man and youth of the village is assigned a very specific duty, which must be performed precisely or the hunt can fail. Scouts are sent out to locate the buffalo. Then lookouts are posted on distant hills to make sure their enemies will not attack while they are busy with the hunt. When everyone is in place, a few men cautiously separate several hundred animals from the immense herd. By occasionally allowing themselves to be seen, these scouts pressure the animals to move towards a narrow ridge. Hidden along that ridge are men and boys who, when the time is right, will stand, shout and wave blankets, forcing the animals along the ridge. Many buffalo escape by doubling back, but for some, the whooping and waving men will create a higher level of fear. These animals will mass together and surge forward. The ridge is chosen because it ends abruptly at a steep cut bank of a small prairie stream. There the mass of the herd forces many over the steep edge. As the animals stumble and cascade down in a frenzy of lethal movements, other men hidden in the ravine appear with stone tipped spears. The vast majority of the huge animals are not chosen by Brother Buffalo to serve his human brothers. These bounce and roll down the escarpment, stand and no worse for their ordeal, calmly trot off. A small number, maybe a dozen, are dazed, injured or stuck in the mud near the river. The men with the spears approach quickly and sever the tendons of the hind legs. When the animals have struggled to exhaustion, the men return for the coup de grace.

Brother Buffalo had been particularly generous to the People. It was extraordinary when the success of the first drive was repeated. The men, women, children and dogs all strained under the load of meat, skins and tallow on the return trek. They had been back to the village for several days already, but for some reason White Hair still felt tired. Below him the sun was now shining on the village and he could see many men and women busying themselves with their chores. Feeling slightly guilty, he rose and began to wind his way back to the village.

When he arrived at his door, his wife gave him a sweet smile and gently pushed him through the doorway. She had sensed his fatigue and had been pampering him the last few days.

"Sit down my man," she said, "I have a warm breakfast for you".

As he settled onto a pile of blankets, she handed him a wooden bowl of hot broth. He sipped it contentedly. When he finished, he lay down for a moment, but soon realized it was a much too lovely day to stay inside. He gathered a few tools and went outside to sit on the sunny side of his house. There he busied himself with one of his favorite tasks, putting the final touches on new arrows. As he worked, he silently prayed. He made prayers of thanksgiving, for he truly had everything he needed. He made prayers of blessing, because he wanted others to have what he had. And he made prayers of invocation, where he asked Wah'Kon-Tah to guide him on the path of honor and wisdom. Sometimes the power of his prayers was so strong that he began to sing quietly aloud. He was so intent on his work that he didn't notice that Grandfather Sun had moved, leaving him sitting in the shade of his house. He was using a small chewed stick to paint three black concentric rings around the shaft of each arrow near the feathers, when an unexpected voice spoke to him.

"It appears my old friend is still losing arrows in the woods."

"No'n-Ce-Tonkah!", White Hair exclaimed as he rose to embrace his friend. "It's good to see you."

Even though White Hair and his friend, Big Heart, lived in different villages, they maintained a friendship which had begun as young men. In their youth, they often traveled together on extended hunts for grizzly bear and even now met annually for a spring dear hunt. That meeting was still months off, so this visit was a special surprise.

Since it was well past midday, White Hair led his friend to the sunny side of the house and laid down a rug for them to recline upon. Within a short time warm food and drink were brought and the guest was honored in the traditional way. When the meal was over a favorite pipe was brought from the house. White Hair slowly filled it with tobacco and placed a small glowing coal in the bowl. Taking six quick puffs, with a quiet voice he offered a prayer to be carried by the sacred smoke to heaven. Then he passed the pipe to his friend. As they smoked, they exchanged news of friends and family. White Hair spoke with some pride about the successful buffalo hunt. The two friends found it easy to sit and let the afternoon slip away. When Grandfather Sun was about a palm width above the ridge, Big Heart stood and spoke.

"Paw-Hiu-Skah", he said. "Pick up those new arrows. I believe that soon a young buck will be moving across that ridge and the tender meat from his loin is what we should have for supper."

White Hair resisted. He pointed out that there was plenty to eat in the village. Even now the women were cooking a rich stew of buffalo, wild potatoes and primrose roots. "Sit my friend. We will have one more smoke; I will tell you another story and we can pull these robes around our shoulders because the air is becoming cool."

Big Heart would not sit down. "Friend, I have noticed today that you seem tired. When you spoke of your buffalo hunt, you used words like work, security, success and comfort. Not once did you express the joy of seeing the beauty of nature. Not once did you thank Brother Buffalo for offering himself to your family. If Wah'Kon-Tah did not believe that you walk through his universe in a sacred manner you would not have success and comfort. Stand my brother and come with me into the woods. Pay your respects to the gifts Wah'Kon-Tah has to offer you."

"No'n-Ce-Tonkah, you are right." Quietly they gathered their bows and arrows. White Hair gave his wife a quick embrace, grabbed a leather jacket, then he and his friend started up the ridge.

About half way up, they paused to discuss strategy. After considering the light and wind, they made their plan. Since White Hair was completely familiar with this ridge, it was decided that he would proceed to a small hunting blind on the north end. Big Heart would swing to the south and try to move any game toward White Hair.

Within a short time, White Hair was crouching comfortably in his hidden hunting spot. Time passed pleasantly. He was well entertained by two squirrels as they leaped and bounded about the leaves in an open area just before him. To his right the huge orange ball of Grandfather Sun approached Mother Earth. A pink and purple wash began to develop over a few western clouds. "We are going to have a beautiful sunset", thought White Hair. He began a quiet prayer of thanksgiving for a wonderful day. Hearing the two squirrels fussing in the trees, made him realize that he had made a stupid mistake—he had allowed his attention to drop for the last several minutes. At an excruciatingly slow rate he turned his head to the south and his eyes locked with two big brown eyes of a small antlered buck. They both froze. The deer stood facing him in the clearing. Within a moment the deer's behavior relaxed. He did not know that he was being watched. White Hair did not move, but the knot in his brain loosened. He knew Brother Deer was still willing to offer himself.

The young buck approached a small sapling within easy bow shot of White Hair's position. There he began to rub his antlers on the small tree. The young buck became engrossed in polishing his rack. While the buck was engaged in this ritual, White Hair slowly changed his position. His left arm was now fully outstretched and the notched arrow had been pulled about half way to his face. Suddenly the mood changed. For no apparent reason the buck was now frozen, head erect, standing in full profile to White Hair. One brown eye seemed to be burning a hole into the blind where White Hair was hidden. The white, warning-flag tail waved partially erect. Two hearts pounded together in the woods. White Hair knowing he must now take his shot, completed his pull and let the arrow fly. The arrow zipped forward and passed harmlessly over the shoulder of the deer. Uncertain what had happened, but knowing he did not like it; the young buck's tail went fully erect. He snorted one loud "har-rumph" and sprang away.

White Hair peered after the deer with a feeling of aggravation. He had made two mistakes he hadn't made since he was a boy. He had allowed his attention to wander and he had become too excited at the moment he fired his arrow. After a few minutes his disappointment began to diminish. He realized Big Heart had been right. This was exactly what he needed. This had been the most exciting moments in a hunt he had experienced for years. His youthful mistakes were the result of youthful exuberance. His friend would enjoy hearing his story.

The light in the woods was beginning to soften and White Hair figured he should go find his arrow. As he prepared to step from the blind, he heard the heavy beat of wings approaching the clearing. Just above the top of the trees, four turkeys glided in at a low angle. One tom landed squarely in the middle of the clearing, just a short distance from the tree where the buck had stood. He shook his feathers about, settled down and began to pick through the fine grass. White Hair smiled. Tom Turkey had saved the life of the young buck and was now offering himself to his human brother. This time, pulling and firing his bow would be more difficult because he had no arrow notched. Turkey are even more sensitive to their surroundings than deer and so White Hair took a full ten minutes to move an arrow to his bow, position himself and draw back. Now the tom was some distance away but he knew he could still make the shot. Clearing his mind, he let the arrow fly. It hit the turkey at the base of the neck.

At that moment, pandemonium broke loose. The other turkeys took off with loud pounding wings. The wounded tom was heading into the woods, thrashing wildly through the underbrush. White Hair, fearing that the wound might not be fatal, leaped to his feet and raced towards his prey. When he was within a few feet,

White Hair sprung forward and tackled the big bird. At that moment a fierce death struggle began. Although seriously wounded, the bird beat and clawed violently at the head and arms of his assailant. White Hair, not wanting the animal to escape or suffer unnecessarily, tried to break its neck. It refused to submit, and White Hair realizing he needed to react quickly, reached to his belt, removed a small hatchet and with one blow ended the struggle.

White Hair rose and checked himself for injuries. He had an ugly scratch on one arm and the sleeve of his jacket was torn. He was bruised, but fine. As he knelt down to pick up the big bird, he felt a flush of pride pass over him. Brother Turkey and been a valiant warrior. With a prayer, he thanked him for giving his life. By the time he had gathered his bow and arrows, Big Heart appeared in the clearing.

They spoke briefly about the details of the hunt as they began walking home. Later tonight the story would be repeated in great detail. White Hair, the successful hunter, would tell the story, but he would honor his friend by describing the care used to guide the game to him. When they exited the woods, they paused for a moment near a large rock jutting from the ridge above the village. Several fires glowed among the homes below. The village looked warm and secure. Suddenly, White Hair remembered the arrow which overshot the deer.

"My friend", he said. "I forgot to pick up my first arrow. I think there's still enough light. I'll go back and see if I can find it." He handed the turkey to Big Heart and turned to retrace his steps alone.

When he arrived at the clearing, a rich golden glow bathed the landscape. He stood at the blind and sighted the flight of his arrow. He walked past were the deer had stood and proceeded into the woods. He traced his steps back and forth several times believing he would soon spot the arrow. The golden glow began to fade. A remarkable stillness descended over the woods. There were no creatures, no wind, only the quiet steps of the hunter moving back and forth. The oak trees around him became sacred. Their tall, dark, straight trunks seemed to be yearning to touch Wah'Kon-Tah. Finally, on one of his return surveys, he saw the notched end of his arrow sticking out of the leaves on the ground. His three black lines of ownership were clearly visible. He placed one knee on the ground and reached for the shaft. At the instant his hand touched the feathers tied to the end, the clearing before him underwent a transformation. The landscape was bathed in the bright light of a snowy midwinter's day. The autumn leaves which he had seen a second before were now covered under nearly a foot of glistening snow. Snow was piled gently on each tree branch. Moving noisily through this scene were two families. Two old men were leading children and grandchildren to a favorite sledding spot. To White Hair the families seemed familiar. He stared intently at the old men. He suddenly recognized them as his own two boys, now grown old with families of their own. In the instant this realization came to him, the scene changed. Now the sunny clearing was damp from a recent springtime rain. Two pretty girls were walking through the clearing. Their manner of dress suggests they might be from his village, but he did not recognize them. Both had baskets filled with morel mushrooms. When they passed the scene changed again. Now it was green summer and another family appeared carrying containers of blackberries. These people were unlike any he had seen before. The man was a hairy creature with thick facial hair and eyebrows. The children were pale and had hair the color of dry grass. Their clothes were strange and brightly colored. They sang a strange song as they passed. As White Hair's mind raced with fear, suddenly it was autumn again. As he looked across the clearing, he saw a young buck. It was similar to the one seen earlier. Just past the deer, White Hair observed a hunter, dressed in speckled clothing, perched in a tree near where the blind had been. The hunter had his bow drawn and in an instant the arrow flew at the deer. As before, the arrow overshot and struck the dirt at White Hair's knee. As the deer fled, White Hair leaped back in fear. The strange shaft was at his feet. He pulled it from the rich soil. A straighter, lighter arrow he had never seen. To his experienced eye, the head appeared so lethal he resisted the urge to touch it. With the arrow cradled in both hands, White Hair stood and looked at the stranger in the tree. For an instant their eyes met. Now, with the arrow firmly grasped in his right hand, he extended his arm as if to offer it back to the distant hunter. The hunter raised his hand in acknowledgment. White Hair's gaze returned to the magnificent arrow and in an instant it transformed to his familiar arrow. He looked for the hunter but now he was alone in his woods.

Shaken by what he had seen, White Hair stood rigidly. In his mind he began to repeat what he had witnessed. Suddenly, he raised his arms to the sky and threw back his head. In a loud, clear voice he began a joyful prayer of thanksgiving to Wah'Kon-Tah. He knew he had been granted a great vision. The bounty and joy of living with Mother Earth would be known by countless generations to come. The feelings which were deep in his heart for this place would, in the future, dwell in the hearts of many more. As his joyful song rolled over the hillsides it seemed to echo on—forever and ever.

Appendix

Cather, Willa. "The Enchanted Bluff" *24 Stories.*
New York: Meridian Classic, 1974, pp. 249-260.
(This short story is about six boys and their love of
a river.)

Catlin, George. *Notes and Letters on the North
American Indians.* Dover Publishing, New York,
1973, pp. 173-175. (This excerpt deals with his
experience of losing his canoe while floating the
Mississippi River.)

DeVoto, Benard. *The Journals of Lewis and Clark.*
New York: Houghton Mifflin, 1953. pp. 189-203.
(These journal entries deal with meeting the
Shoshone Indians.)

Longfellow, Henry, Wadsworth. *Song of Hiawatha.*
New York: Hurst and Co., 1898. pp. 87-97. (This
is the chapter entitled, "Hiawatha's Fishing". It is
the story of Hiawatha's epic battle with Nahma,
the giant sturgeon.)

Neihardt, John, G. *Black Elk Speaks.* Lincoln,
Nebraska, University of Nebraska Press, 1979. pp.
1-6. (This is the first chapter of the book where
Black Elk ceremonially lights the peace pipe and
prays at the beginning of telling his life's story.)